THE PARIS AFFAIR

AFFAIRS OF THE HEART, VOLUME 1

KRISTI LEA

First Printing, 2011

ISBN 978-0-9982045-3-6

www.KristiLea.com

Acknowledgements

To my mom, thank you for a lifetime of support and encouragement, first in reading books and now in writing them.

Thank you especially to Amanda Berry, Dawn Blankenship, Jeannie Lin, and Shawntelle Madison for your weekly kick in the pants, your lack of sympathy for my complaints, and your honesty, support and optimism.

Chapter 1

She was new to the building and a blonde. Helmut always noticed the blondes. Especially the long-legged ones.

She sat on one of the brown leather armchairs in the corner of the ground-floor Starbucks, calmly sipping steaming liquid with ruby-red plump lips. Kissable lips. Her long legs were crossed primly at the knee, but her skirt had ridden up, revealing a tempting glimpse of shapely thighs. One high-heeled pump dangled from her raised toe, playfully.

Helmut slid his laptop bag to the floor in front of him and surreptitiously studied her as he added sugar and a splash of milk to his coffee. Her hair color looked natural, or else a very expensive salon job. Platinum highlights around her face accentuated a golden tan that was slightly pink around the temples. He could picture her sunning herself on a beach, bikini top unhooked while he massaged tropical-scented oil into her supple skin.

The image sent a jolt of raw lust shooting through his veins, and he gave himself a mental shake. He needed to clean the cobwebs out of his brain, not waste all of his mental power mooning over a woman. No matter how delectable her tongue looked as it tasted her coffee.

Focus, Helmut.

He wondered where she worked and hoped it wasn't his department. The company had strict policies about "fraternization," especially when one employee held a position of power over the other. Executives were not allowed to date their secretaries. Not anymore.

Executives and power reminded Helmut of why he was in the office before seven a.m. instead of recovering from his trip. Midnight flights and predawn phone calls did not mix well.

The woman set down her coffee and unfurled the pages of this morning's Tribune. The business section.

Helmut capped his coffee and slipped on a cardboard sleeve. His assistant was already waiting for him upstairs, ready to fill him in on the upheaval in the company hierarchy from the past two days. The bank of elevators was back and to his left.

What the hell. May as well start the day with a little fun. It's all downhill from here. Helmut turned right.

He slung his bag back over one shoulder, loosened his tie a touch, setting it slightly askew. He reached his hand up and brushed the hair above his forehead —just where a small streak of gray had appeared over the last year — knocking a strand out of place. Perfect.

Helmut picked up his coffee, hunched his shoulders slightly, and walked over to the blonde, wearing the boyish grin that so many women had been unable to resist.

"Excuse me, miss?"

The blonde looked up, dazzling him with eyes like the Caribbean at dawn. His mouth went dry and he nearly tripped over his next words.

"I wonder if you could help me a minute."

She sat her cup down on the side table and studied him, her appraisal cool. She was a little older than he had first guessed, probably late twenties or maybe thirty. Her eyes were too knowing and her face too refined to be a college intern or fresh-faced secretary. Even better.

"I am meeting my new boss in a few minutes, and I want to make a good impression. How do I look? Is my tie straight?" Helmut tried to make his voice sound a little helpless, like a bachelor in sore need of a woman's guidance.

"Your tie is a little crooked." Her voice was low and smooth, sexy.

Helmut felt a tightening in his groin, and wanted to hear that voice say his name. He reached one hand up to fix his tie, deliberately knocking it off center the other way. "How is this?"

She glanced at her watch, then stood. "Here, allow me."

Her expression was polite, but her voice held a hint of amusement. As she stepped closer to Helmut, her scent filled his nostrils, light and fruity with a hint of coconut. He held still and as her fingers brushed his lapels, deftly adjusting his tie.

"Much appreciated. My name is Helmut, by the way, Helmut Forrester. And you are?" He reached out his right hand. She gave it a quick, businesslike shake.

Those beautiful blue eyes were wide, and her fingers were cool to the touch. Too cool. He usually knew when a woman was attracted to him, but this time he sensed nerves more than lust. Disappointment hit him in the gut, and lower.

"Claire." She looked down at her hand, and carefully extracted it from his grasp. "Now, if you'll excuse me, Helmut Forrester, I have to go."

Helmut watched her walk calmly toward the bank of elevators, her posture confident, hips swaying lightly.

"Geez, Helmut, lighten up. I said I'd have the revenue numbers done today. It's only eight thirty." Ben Lackey reclined back in the boardroom chair, juggling a small stress ball.

"Which means I have two hours before I have to stand up before the new CEO and explain them. Is the project even in the black?" Helmut snaked one hand out and caught the lightweight ball mid-flight and set it carefully down on the table.

Ben straightened. "Don't you trust me? We've been friends for what, fifteen years now? What crawled up your ass this morning?"

"I think it started with a five a.m. phone call informing me that Sheffield was retiring, and his kid was taking over the company."

"Afraid the 'kid' will take you down a notch, oh holy CFO?"

Helmut tossed the ball back at his long-time friend.

Ben ducked and it hit the wall behind him with a soft thud. The ball rolled under the table and bumped into the shoe of one of the regional sales directors. The woman picked it up and handed it back to Helmut with a quirked eyebrow.

Ben snickered. "How was Palm Beach?"

"The same as always." Helmut hadn't seen so much as a grain of sand. His mother's house — his childhood home — was in West Palm Beach, thirty minutes from the shore. After she broke her leg last month, Helmut had been pressing his mom to move to a retirement community. Not even assisted living, just a place with a community. Friends. Someone to talk to.

"If all those beach bunnies couldn't help you unwind..." Ben wagged his eyebrows up and down.

"There wasn't much time for checking out the 'local wildlife,' Ben. Familial responsibility. You wouldn't understand." He spent the week alternately chauffeuring her to doctor appointments and standing on one ladder or another, repairing and repainting her house.

"Oh, I totally understand," said Ben with mock seriousness. "All of the time you spend crunching numbers has deflated your, er, confidence with the ladies."

"Hmph." Helmut knew why Ben was egging him on. As the two perennial bachelors of the company, they had always jokingly compared their dating track records. Helmut had hit a dry spot the past six months since his promotion, and he knew Ben couldn't resist rubbing it in.

"Come on, old man," Ben continued. "Admit it. Your glory days are long gone. Soon you'll be scoping out the old folks homes, asking hunched old biddies to rub you down with Vicks Vapo-Rub."

Helmut twisted his lips into what he hoped passed for a smile. The image would have been funnier if he didn't have a stack of retirement community brochures still left to unpack from his suitcase. "There was a hot blonde down in the coffee shop this morning who was checking me out. If I hadn't been in such a rush to cover for your sorry ass in the presentations today, I might have let her ask me out."

Ben sat up straighter. "Hot blonde? About five-eight? Skirt suit? No pantyhose?"

The boardroom was beginning to fill up with the other high-ranking executives. James Sheffield, the retiring CEO, would be arriving any minute to make the official announcement.

As his peers began to file in, Helmut lowered his voice a notch. "You know her?"

"Maybe." Ben rubbed his chin thoughtfully. "You think you could score with her?"

"Sure." Helmut conjured the image of those plump lips. The pink tongue. It was a pleasant fantasy anyway.

Ben's eyes flicked around the room and he leaned in. "Care to make a wager on it?"

"Still sore you lost the last one to me? About your hunting cabin versus my beach house?"

"I didn't lose. It's all in how you interpret the numbers."

"And we both know who's better with numbers." Helmut reached into his suit pocket and withdrew a pen. He set it gently on the table in front of him, next to the manila folder his secretary had given him.

"You gonna put your money where your mouth is, or what?"

"Whatever. Fifty bucks she goes out with me." Helmut nodded to the Vice President of their European division from across the room. He hadn't known Pierre was in the States this week. How much notice did the rest of the company get about today?

"Penny ante. I lost five hundred bucks to you over my mountain hideaway."

"It's not my fault the ladies prefer long walks on the beach to hiking in the mud."

Helmut flipped open the folder, and scanned the latest quarterly report. As the CFO of Sheffield & Fox, he would be expected to present the current numbers to their new CEO, CJ Sheffield, son of the newly retired James Sheffield. That was the thirty-second overview his secretary, Betty, had given him over the phone this morning.

"A thousand." Ben's voice was practically a whisper. "You've got two weeks."

"Think I can't get a date in two weeks? How washed up do you think I am?"

"Not just a date. I'm talking carnal knowledge. And for that kind of money, I want proof."

Helmut weighed the wager. He'd tossed it out as a joke, but Ben looked serious. A thousand dollars was a relatively small amount compared to the hefty salary his new title afforded him. A salary that he knew Ben envied. Not that Ben's was paltry by any stretch of the imagination.

If Helmut lost, then Ben could gloat for weeks, or longer. That would be better than all of the accountant jokes and workaholic cracks he'd been putting up with lately. And if he won...he pictured the woman's silky blond hair, and wondered if it was as soft to the touch as it had looked.

"Deal."

"Have you met the new CEO yet?" asked Ben.

Helmut shook his head.

He hadn't had a chance to talk to the new guy, but he'd heard a few snatches of gossip already this morning. His new boss had been a rising star at his previous post. He'd taken an Internet startup from his friend's garage to a multi-million dollar corporation in under six years.

Sheffield & Fox was a completely different sort of business. Stable, reliable, set in its ways. All of the flash and hype of the Internet wouldn't help the kid negotiate with employees who had worked the same job since the Kennedy era. He was in for a rude awakening. Hell of a time for James to retire.

The low murmur of whispers, shuffling papers, and the faint beeping of cell phones hushed to an expectant silence as James Sheffield entered the door at the far end of the room and stepped up to the podium. Helmut quickly set his own phone on vibrate as his boss and mentor stepped up to the microphone.

"Ladies and Gentlemen, allow me to present your new Chief Executive Officer, Claire James Sheffield." The room erupted in polite applause as a long-legged blonde stepped to her father's side.

"Shit," Helmut muttered under his breath and glanced back at Ben.

Ben grinned wolfishly.

Chapter 2

Claire rubbed her temples and wished, for the nine thousandth time today, that she had worn her glasses instead of contacts. She blinked twice, attempting to focus on the circle of suits sitting around the small conference room table. She glanced surreptitiously down at her agenda. The manufacturing department. Only two more meet-and-greets left: Finance and Law.

"...are proud to report that productivity has been increasing steadily since the inception of our new Streamlined Engineering Process," Ingrid, the regional director, was saying.

Claire schooled her features into what she hoped passed for an interested expression and tried to pay attention. The last guy had droned on for fifteen minutes about the technical minutiae of various models of engine components in Sheffield & Fox's product line. Technology was not her forte—business, strategic direction, and people were. But it was only a matter of time, she knew, before she would be speaking the lingo as well.

Claire hadn't known a web server from a cocktail waitress before she and her then-boyfriend, Frank, had founded Arachnava ten years ago. Frank had been the technical genius, and Claire didn't need to know how all the software was created to help drive the business strategy.

Even after their personal relationship soured last year, they remained business partners until Frank wanted to take the company down a riskier path. One Claire wanted no part of. When the rest of the board—comprised heavily of Frank's college classmates—agreed, she sold her shares and bailed.

Her retirement had lasted a whopping three weeks before her father called. Saturday afternoon—was it only two days ago? He simply informed her of her new position. And, like every other demand her father had ever made of her during the past thirty-four years of her life, she obeyed.

She thought she had long since moved past trying to please the stubborn old man. Or to make him proud of her. Pride was something he reserved for his sons: Chris, the surgeon, and Caleb, the judge. Not for her.

Father must have been desperate to dump the company this fast, and on Claire of all people. Was it his health? Her stepmother's health? James had denied both. But he wouldn't explain his reasons, and that irked Claire. She hated to walk into any job unprepared. And she was afraid of what might be lurking under the veneer of Sheffield & Fox's shiny corporate office.

Claire shifted her attention back to the meeting. The department heads were done speaking, and everyone stood to leave. She politely shook hands, repeating names she had memorized when they were introduced. She was exceptionally thankful for that useful skill.

Claire turned to her executive assistant. "What's next, Steph?"

She and Steph had been friends for a long time. Steph's organizational skills plus Claire's instincts for business strategies made a lethal combination. Lethal for their competition. Getting her on board at Sheffield and Fox, and with a hefty raise, was Claire's one prerequisite to accepting the position.

"Finance has their own conference room up on the fourteenth floor." Steph glanced down at Claire's high-heeled pumps. "Stairs or elevator?"

"Stairs. I'll do it barefoot if I have to. My calves are cramping from these heels. I think one of my first acts as CEO will be to implement a casual dress code."

Steph led the way out of the conference room and down a short corridor to the fire stairs. Once on the landing, Claire slipped off her shoes and wiggled bare toes on the gray rubber floor.

"Actually, the official dress code is already casual."

Claire looked envyingly at her friend's sporty brown leather flats.

"But upper management is traditional."

"And there's no way they'll take me seriously wearing jeans and tennis shoes." Claire filled in what Steph had left unspoken. "Especially at my age."

Steph's eyes twinkled. "Three floors up."

Claire grinned. "I'll race you."

"Better not. I won't be able to brief you on the next bunch of guys when you're thirty feet below me." Steph grinned back and started up the stairs at an easy pace.

Claire caught up in three steps. "How many are in the next meeting?"

"Five. Jim Flanders heads up auditing. Marcy Robinson from contracts. Pete Sampson is the controller. Betty Krank is the executive assistant to the CFO—"

"Helmut Forrester," supplied Claire. "We met."

"I didn't think you had time to talk to anyone after the press conference this morning." Steph had already rounded the landing and was two steps up the next flight.

"We met in the coffee shop before work. He hit on me."

"Oh." Steph chuckled. "Oh no. What is he like?"

Beautiful green eyes. Broad shoulders. Nice smile. "Not bad looking, but the come-on was totally corny. He asked me to straighten his tie. Had no clue who I was."

Steph giggled outright. "Figures. He has a bit of a reputation around here. As a playboy. Or heartbreaker, depending on how sappy you are about that sort of thing."

Just like my ex, but this one doesn't hide his philandering. "Lovely. Just what I need in my executive team."

"As long as he keeps his pants on in the boardroom, you'll be fine."

Steph was almost half a flight above already, and Claire had to hurry to catch up.

"Your father thinks pretty highly of him. In fact, gossip has it that he should have been next in line for your father's job. Your job, I mean."

"Even better. Keep your ears open on this guy, Steph. I don't want anyone spreading rumors about him—or me—as revenge for my getting promoted over him."

"I'm way ahead of you, boss." Steph pushed open the stairwell door. Claire paused on the landing and slipped her shoes back on. She took a steadying breath and stepped into the brightly lit hallway.

Helmut checked his reflection in the mirror at the back of his bookshelf. He straightened his tie, then ducked down to check his hair around the mementos lined up across the front of the shelf.

This morning's meeting in the coffee shop with Claire Sheffield hadn't gone badly. Exactly. But that was before he knew she was James' daughter. And his new boss.

"Meeting time." Betty stood by the door to his office.

Helmut patted his suit pocket to check for his cell phone, and grabbed a leather bound folio from the console. He didn't have to ask whether Betty had the meeting room prepared and the presentation loaded up on the display. She knew her job and executed it with efficiency.

"How is your mother doing?" she asked.

"Stubborn as ever."

"I don't blame her, you know. She's only a few years older than I am."

Helmut stepped ahead of her and opened the door to the south wing. "I just wish she'd listen to my advice on this. That house is huge. And with Dad gone, my brother off in God knows which jungle this month, and my baby sister almost out of college, it's too much for one woman alone. She would have so much more freedom in one of those nice retirement villages. Hell, some of them look more like all-inclusive resorts than apartments."

Betty fixed him with a pointed look as she walked through the open door. "You are talking about the home she's lived in for over forty years now."

"One that's full of nothing but dust."

"And memories."

Memories and dust and ghosts. *Sometimes the past is better left behind us, not clouding the air we breathe every day.* He kept the thought to himself.

Betty paused outside the conference room door. "Are you ready?"

"As ever."

Through the patterned glass of the door, he could see a yellow blob that must be Claire's sun-kissed blond hair. He steeled himself, putting on his best game face.

Helmut took a seat at one end of the oblong table. The first of the three speakers jumped right into his presentation. They were all his direct reports, and he'd okayed their material an hour ago. With Claire's focus on the screen at the other end, he was free to study her without her noticing.

After this morning's press conference, and Ben's little surprise about the identity of the coffee shop woman, Helmut had looked for Claire Sheffield's official press release bio. The standard publicity blurb focused mainly on her education and years at Arachnava. There was no husband listed and no ring on her left hand. His bet was still safe in that regard. The hobbies listed were the normal executive stuff, tennis and golf. He was going to have to dig a little deeper to find just the right hook. Every woman had a weakness. Roses, motorcycles, beach getaways. Once he uncovered Claire's, she was his.

"Helmut, you're up," Jim said as he returned to his seat.

"Thanks." Helmut stood with a confident smile. "First, I want to say 'Welcome Aboard,' Claire. I know I speak for all of us when I say that I am looking forward to working with you. I trust your first impressions of us have been favorable so far?"

Claire smiled her coolly amused smile. "Thank you, Helmut. I am already enjoying working with you all. And as for first impressions..."

She paused.

"I have already been made to feel *useful*. I look forward to continuing to serve my colleagues and this company."

Helmut didn't miss the way Claire's eyes twinkled. Whether his shenanigans this morning had gained or cost him ground remained to be seen.

Helmut launched into his presentation, covering in depth his short- and long-term strategies. He talked mainly toward Claire and her assistant, knowing his own guys were well briefed on his plans, and on the bottom line.

"Could you go back to the previous slide, please, Betty?" interrupted Claire.

Helmut paused mid-thought and nodded at Betty. Behind him, the wall glowed white with columns of red and black numbers from their aircraft division. "Did you have a question?"

Claire craned her neck to the side, and Helmut realized his shadow was blocking part of the screen. Obligingly, he stepped out of the way of the projector. He studied her profile while she studied the numbers. Her nose was fine and high, neck long and slender. A curl of her hair was tucked behind one ear, and Helmut wondered how she would taste if he nibbled that sensitive spot. Like coconuts, maybe.

"Yes, I do have a question. The Shadow Fly project."

He blinked, startled at the direction his mind had wandered. "It is our first military project. I'm sure manufacturing will be happy to explain—"

"I am familiar with it. My father is very proud to be producing motors for the new unmanned helicopters that the military wants. But—"

Helmut glanced looked back at the numbers on the screen. Ben had assured him after the press conference this morning that the numbers were fine. They weren't. The bottom line was red. Hell, half the lines were red. More than half.

"Why is it losing so much money?" The chill in her voice was nothing compared to the hot resentment smoldering in the pit of his stomach at having been caught off guard. In front of her.

Helmut gave a deliberately casual shrug and tried to explain the discrepancy away. "Startup costs, mainly. The beginning of any new project is always—"

"Betty, flip back three more slides. Yes, that one. Could you please explain to me how you can predict a revenue stream like this one, with such a large loss on the books?"

He had looked at the reports right before his vacation. Reports Ben had provided. And Helmut had signed off on them then. Ben always produced what he predicted. Always. How could things have changed so drastically in one week?

"Yes, well, you might have a point. It does look like our forecast is a bit more optimistic than today's numbers seem to indicate..."

"Did your analysis not take into account the startup costs? We've been in this business for forty years. There ought to have been plenty of historical data to use for the estimates."

Claire uncrossed her legs and shifted in her seat. The motion distracted him for half a second, and he couldn't help noticing her tuck her bare feet beneath her. He could just make out the pointed toe of one shoe under the edge of the table. He had to force his gaze from the expanse of her bare legs, and clamp down on the rush of heat that went straight to his cock. He cleared his throat, trying to formulate an answer to her question.

"We do rely heavily on historical data in our estimating process," he said. "If you would allow me a moment to explain. We have twenty-five years of data in the computers to utilize when we bid a contract. But this is the first time we have ever dealt with the US military. We underestimated the overhead of the additional security, background checks, and facility upgrades that need to comply with their terms.

"I am sure the Shadow Fly project manager would be happy to go over this in finer detail than I can provide. Remember, my department only handles the final numbers. Back to where I was, Betty, if you please."

Helmut heard the bitter edge in his own voice and resolved to keep his cool for the remainder of the meeting. He normally kept tabs on all of the major projects, and could explain any of the numbers—good or bad—in more detail than most accountants could. Ben had some serious explaining to do.

Chapter 3

The smell of garlic and pepper assailed Helmut's nostrils the instant the elevator opened, making his stomach growl. He had hoped to leave work two hours ago, and stop by the gym on the way home. Maybe catch the end of the Blackhawks game on ESPN. Instead, the night was serving up takeout and endless spreadsheets.

He nodded to the night guard and grinned at the lanky young deliveryman leaning on the security guard's desk, eyes closed and head bopping to the beat playing on his iPod.

"Still on the evening shift, eh Stevie?"

Stevie grinned back, still bopping his head. He held up one finger. Helmut waited, patiently. He knew the drill.

After ten more seconds, Stevie yanked out his earplugs and rolled his head around, cracking his neck. "Sorry, still working on the last ten measures of that song. *Jesu, Joy of Men's Desiring* snuck in there somehow. My sister's wedding must have infiltrated my mind."

"Is this the last composition for your master's thesis?"

"Yeah, man. I'm cutting it close. The performance is scheduled for the day after tomorrow. You coming?"

"Wouldn't miss it for the world. As long as you didn't forget my wonton soup again."

"I never," said the graduate music student with a dramatic flourish of his hand.

"Just giving you shit. Here, keep the change." Helmut handed over a fifty.

"I can't take that much."

"Sure you can. I don't have anything smaller. Besides, I'm being selfish. If I piss you off and Mr. Hon gives some punk this delivery route, I'll never get a hot crab Rangoon again."

Stevie chuckled. "Thanks, Mr. Forrester. Much appreciated." He handed Helmut a warm paper bag with a menu stapled to the side. "Careful, think the sauce is leaking a bit."

Helmut palmed the bag, turning the greasy splotch away from his tie. He started to walk away, then noticed Stevie plugging his earphones back in.

"You hanging out here tonight?"

"No, another delivery."

Belatedly, Helmut noticed another bag sitting on the desk behind Stevie. He raised one eyebrow. There weren't many people left in the building at this time of night, and he surprised someone else had ordered from such a tiny restaurant twelve blocks away. There were half a dozen Chinese places between here and

Hon's, though none worth mentioning, in his opinion.

"Who's it for?"

"CJ something or other. I guess the guy's new to the building."

Claire. Hon's was one of her father's favorite joints, too. Helmut smiled to himself. After yesterday's disastrous presentation, he'd managed to speak only three words to her. "Good morning, CJ." A little dinner party was just what he needed to start gaining ground.

"That's my new boss. If you don't mind, I'll take it up to her. I needed to drop by her office for a minute anyway. How much is it?" Helmut set his bag back down and pulled out his wallet.

"*Her* office? Your new boss is a chick?"

"I wouldn't call her a 'chick' to her face if you wanted a tip. She's James' daughter."

"No offense intended. But watch out for a lady boss. My advisor's a tough old bat. Keeps me in line better than my own mother."

Helmut handed over another fifty and smiled. "I'll keep that in mind. Take it easy, Stevie."

Helmut hefted both sacks and whistled to himself as he strode back to the elevator. He hadn't been lying about needing to talk to Claire, but he didn't know she was working late.

After hours of catching up on the email he'd missed on vacation, he had just started digging into the preliminary results of the yearly financial audit. Had James still been in charge, Helmut would have been in his office going over the results together. Not because Helmut needed James' guidance, but because he always kept his boss in the loop.

There was a conference call scheduled with the auditors on Wednesday, and they had requested the CEO's presence. Helmut wanted to triple check all of his own reports before calling Claire. He had intended to email her tonight and set up a quick face-to-face before the call. Bringing her dinner would be much cozier.

Carefully juggling both bags, Helmut knocked on the CEO's office door. It was open a crack, yellow light spilling out into the dimly lit hallway.

"Room Service," he called out as he gently pushed open the door.

Helmut looked around. At first glance, the office was empty. The dark paneled space had been James' power center for Helmut's entire seventeen-year career here. He could still remember when he was first hired, right out of college, and had greeted the intimidating older man with a sweaty handshake and a lot of "Yes, sir" and "No, sir". Over the past few years, he'd spent more time in meetings up here than anywhere else in the building, except his own office on the floor below.

"Hello?" he asked again and turned to leave.

"Do you cook, too?"

Claire was sitting cross-legged in the overstuffed brown leather sofa. She was small compared to the scale of the thing. With her blond hair tucked behind her ears, she looked very girlish. And then she unfolded her long legs and stood.

His eyes traveled upward from her feet to gently curved hips and a slender waistline. She wore the slacks from today's black pantsuit but had removed the jacket, and her silk blouse hugged pertly rounded breasts. Very grown-up breasts. He cleared his throat.

"I do. Cook, that is. If I'm desperate." He held up the sacks. "I guess we both ordered from the same Chinese joint. Would you care for some company?"

Claire yawned, covering her mouth delicately with one hand. She actually blushed. "Sorry about that. I've been going over last quarter's project reports all evening."

"Heh. That will put you to sleep in a hurry."

"No, they're all very educational. I'm not used to sitting still for so long."

Helmut looked around. The only spot on the huge mahogany desk not covered with printouts held her laptop. "Understandable. Where would you like me to put this?"

"Over here on the coffee table would be great. Thanks, Helmut." The coffee table was piled with notebooks and file folders, too.

Her hair had been down but carefully styled earlier in the day, but she had drawn it back into a loose ponytail. A long strand had escaped the band and curled around the back of her ear while she bent over the piles, stacking things to clear a corner of the table. The tips of her ears were flushed pink despite the chill of the office. Another blush? She motioned for him to set down the bag, and moved an armful of notebooks to the desk.

"Mind if I join you? We can make it a working dinner. I wanted to show you my notes for tomorrow's conference call."

She turned then, and he saw a flicker of something in her eyes before she schooled her features into a smooth, cool façade. Uncertainty or calculation. Maybe both. He could work with either.

"That would be nice."

Helmut smiled. "Great. I'll be right back with my notes."

Claire laughed so hard at Helmut's story about the dog riding sidecar on its geriatric owner's motorcycle that she let a piece of shrimp slide off of her chopsticks. It landed with a wet squish in the paperboard box, splatting her blouse with Kung Pao sauce.

She set down her chopsticks and grabbed a paper napkin to blot the mess.

"Let me help with that." Helmut jumped to his feet.

Claire watched as he strolled over to the mini-bar refrigerator her father had installed along one wall of bookshelves. She had no business checking out her CFO's butt. No matter how firm his ass looked, or how toned the muscles of his thighs beneath the smooth gray fabric. She was a firm believer in casual dress, but tailored wool slacks did hang especially nice from some men's backsides.

Helmut turned back around, a clear plastic bottle in one hand, and Claire quickly looked back down at the greasy splotch on her top. She hoped that he attributed the hot flush of her cheeks to laughter.

"Club soda." He wet a napkin with the bottle. "It's a lifesaver in emergencies like this."

He stood close to her, and she smelled faint traces of juniper and rosewood and something deeper that was primal and male. His scent shot a desire of heat through her, pooling in the pit of her stomach. And between her legs.

Helmut touched the napkin to a tendril of her hair, gently cleaning off the sauce. The slight motion sent sparkles down her scalp. Then he lowered his hand and touched it to her stomach.

The cool liquid soaked through her blouse jolting her temporarily befuddled senses into awareness, tightening her nipples into hard nubs.

She snatched the napkin from his fingers. "I can do that."

Helmut shrugged and sat back down on the chair across from her while Claire concentrated on blotting her blouse. It gave her an excuse to focus her eyes somewhere away from his hands. Strong, capable hands.

Nimble fingers.

She patted the stain a few more times for good measure.

"My dry cleaner won't fire me after all." She set the napkin aside. The liquid had left a swatch of the fine silk nearly transparent and clinging to her abdomen. She tucked one arm across her lap self-consciously.

"Happy to be of service." His dark green-gray eyes held a shine that made her shift in her seat, even though his posture was relaxed, easy. He broke a crab Rangoon in half. "I've told you all of my secrets. What about you?"

"I don't have quite the repertoire of anecdotes that you do."

"How about the basics? What do you do for fun?" Helmut took a bite of the Rangoon, leaving her to fill the silence.

"Fun? What's that? I live for my job," she said with only half a laugh.

"Yeah right. Living for your job always gives you a deep bronze tan."

Claire blushed again. "I had a few weeks of downtime after I left my last company. I spent most of it on my bike."

"Motor or foot-powered?"

"Foot-powered. You didn't notice how clueless I was about all the motorcycle stories you've been telling?"

Helmut shrugged. "I didn't see cycling listed on your official company bio."

Claire rolled her eyes. "I think my assistant wrote that for me. Golf and tennis, right? Or did she add 'charity work' this time?"

"Do you actually golf?"

"I can generally hit the ball with a club, sometimes in the right direction, if that's what you mean. Most of the techno-wizards I worked with at my last company didn't play any games that didn't involve a console and a joystick, so I never bothered to work on it. Let me guess, you're a semi-pro?"

"I can keep up, when I have to. When you're the C-F-O and not the C-E-O, your job is to make small talk and not outshine the boss." Something in his tone made Claire shift in her seat again, but the air seemed noticeably cooler than it had a minute a go.

She busied herself closing the lid on her half-eaten dinner and carried it to the same mini-fridge where Helmut had found the club soda.

She shuffled aside cans of soda, beer, and a bottle of wine and settled her takeout in the empty spot, and made a mental note to have the fridge cleaned out. Her father belonged a different generation, where offering a visitor a "drink" implied that alcohol was acceptable during the workday.

Claire dared a look over her shoulder at her dinner guest. Helmut carefully gathered up his own trash, then wiped down the coffee table where they'd eaten. That last touch was way more thoughtful than she would have expected from a guy.

"Now, about the meeting tomorrow." He reached for his laptop, shifting the stacks of notebooks around on the coffee table to make room for it.

Oh yeah, work. Claire glanced at the wall clock. It was nearly eleven. She didn't know if she could concentrate on any more numbers. "Mind if we finish in the morning? I need some sleep tonight if you don't want me snoozing through the conference call."

"Sure. Me, too. I'll stop by at nine tomorrow? Sorry if I let the time get away from us."

The glow in his eyes didn't look sorry at all.

Chapter 4

The concert hall Thursday night was packed with a mix of college students and community members. As the lights dimmed, Helmut scanned the rows of heads in front of him, searching for a familiar blonde.

She was here somewhere. Betty had mentioned it before he left work this afternoon. Sheffield & Fox donated three scholarships to the university every year, one of them in music. James had never taken the time to come to any of the student performances, but Claire must have thought it was important.

Helmut never missed one. Stevie was the best of tonight's performers. He had played one of his pieces solo on the piano during the first half, and he was directing a string quartet for this next piece. The lanky kid stepped up to a podium and began waving his small baton, like a magician with a wand. Helmut closed his eyes and let the music wash over him.

He himself didn't have an ounce of talent, outside of buying a CD or tuning the radio. But he'd seen firsthand how hard music students worked for their degrees, and how little most earned right after graduation. Once his salary surpassed what he needed to live on, he started donating to the university. The past three years, his anonymous checks were enough to pay full tuition for a student. When his favorite Chinese delivery guy mentioned grad school, he sent a note to the admissions director. Not that he would ever admit that to Stevie.

When he invariably ran into acquaintances at these concerts, he always alluded to representing Sheffield & Fox. Claire might know better, but he wasn't worried tonight. Anyone could walk up to the box office and purchase a ticket.

Stevie's last piece ended to a thunderous round of applause. The kid had talent. Helmut had quietly called a business-school buddy of his who was now working for Disney and sent him the home-recorded CD Stevie had given him last semester. He was pretty sure the kid would have his choice of jobs, if he didn't decide to strike out on his own.

The lights came on, and the crowd dispersed into the lobby of the performing arts building. Helmut bought wine in a plastic cup from the concession stand and scanned the room again. The student performers would be out soon, to mingle with their friends and benefactors. And maybe a talent scout or two.

"I didn't know you were a music lover, Helmut."

Claire's honeyed tones teased his senses, and he turned, smiling. "Stevie—the last performer—is our Chinese food delivery man. I promised I'd come watch his big concert."

Claire arched one delicate eyebrow. "You order takeout often?"

Helmut shrugged. "What brings the illustrious Sheffield & Fox CEO to such a pedestrian gathering?"

"I got a personal invitation from the chancellor to meet some of the company's scholarship recipients. It's good PR. The press either ignores us, or gives us only the briefest coverage, and we're having trouble recruiting new-hires lately. I want to turn our reputation around. Get our name out there with a positive message."

"Your father wasn't ever worried about the press."

"James Sheffield and I have differing viewpoints in a number of areas," she said frostily.

Helmut raised his cups to his lips for a sip of the overly sweet red wine, and paused. All the color had drained out of Claire's face.

"What's the matter?" he asked. "You look like you've seen a ghost."

"It's my ex," Claire said.

Frank Burwell met Claire's gaze from across the room, and started immediately toward her. She cringed.

She had heard from a friend that he and his latest girlfriend were on the rocks. The last time he had woman trouble, he had shown up on Claire's doorstep, smelling like rum and looking at Claire with puppy dog eyes. It was the same expression he wore tonight.

She almost had to physically kick him out of her apartment that night, and she didn't relish exchanging *pleasantries* with him again.

"I am sorry," she said to Helmut. "He can be a real jerk. I'll try to get rid of him as quickly as possible."

Helmut nodded, a half-smile on his lips.

"Claire. You look beautiful tonight, sweetheart."

Claire turned and glared. "What do you want, Frank?"

Frank flashed her a hurt expression. With his brushed-back dark hair and longish nose, he looked like a hawk circling his prey. How had she ever found that angular face attractive? "I just wanted to say hello to you, my dear. I have missed your company."

"Your company has missed me, you mean," she muttered under her breath. His stock price was down twenty percent already in the few weeks since she'd left.

"What have you been doing with yourself during your little vacation? You must be getting restless for some real work by now," he asked, missing her backhanded remark.

"Didn't you hear? I took a new position."

Frank looked genuinely startled. "Really? Where?"

"Sheffield & Fox. The board approved me as CEO Sunday afternoon. I started Monday."

His bird-like eyebrows shot up even higher, and Claire felt a surge of triumph. When she'd announced her resignation from Arachnava, Frank had sneered that she'd be back begging for her job in a week.

His eyes narrowed. "Your daddy's company? I thought you said you'd never work for him."

"She doesn't. James retired."

Claire's eyes flew to Helmut's face. His jaw was set in a grim line as he studied Frank.

"Frank, this is Helmut Forrester. Helmut, Frank Burwell."

Helmut swapped his wine glass to his left hand and offered his right to Frank, but the slime ignored it.

Frank drooped his shoulders and flashed his puppy dog look at Claire again. "If you need anything, Claire, I'm here for you. I hope you will always remember that."

She felt the touch of Helmut's hand on the small of her back and looked up. His green eyes twinkled. "The performers are on their way out. Let's go find our scholarship student, shall we? Pleasure to meet you, Burwell."

Claire flashed him a smile and allowed Helmut to lead her to a small group of bright-eyed students, well aware that she had not told Frank that Helmut worked for her. She felt a pang of conscience at deliberately misleading her ex into thinking she had a date. But then, Helmut hadn't volunteered that information either. That was...interesting.

While she complimented performances and posed for a photo with a bashful soprano with the voice of an angel, she could feel Frank's gaze following her. Helmut stuck close to her side, and Claire was grateful for his presence. Frank was not the type to provoke a direct confrontation for any reason. He was too passive-aggressive. It was one of the man's worst traits and top of the list of reasons she'd left him over a year ago. Right after his habit of sleeping with his executive assistants.

As the party began to break up, a few of the horn players decided to give an impromptu encore in the lobby area. Their music was beautiful, but made conversation nearly impossible. The wine she'd downed after the concert had seeped into her bones, relaxing her for the first time all week.

"Shall I call us a cab?" Helmut's lips were a breath away from her earlobe. Claire shivered at the husky timbre of his voice.

She opened her mouth to speak, but she was drowned out by a saxophone's bluesy solo.

Instead, Claire nodded, and soon she was sliding across a rippled vinyl seat to make room for Helmut.

"Where to, folks?"

"Ladies first," Helmut said.

She gave her address to the cabbie. "Thank you for helping me escape Frank."

In the shadows, his dark eyes gleamed like molten lead. "Glad to be *useful*." The darkness couldn't disguise the smile in his voice.

Claire laughed. "Shall we call it even, then?"

"Do women always have to keep score?"

Claire quirked her lips. "I thought men liked everything to be a contest."

Helmut's gaze slipped away for a moment, out to the orange-lit Chicago streets. When he looked back, the streetlights reflected in his eyes like twin fires.

"If this is a sport, then I've scored twice."

Claire arched an eyebrow. "And I thought accountants could add."

Helmut grinned. "First, I succeeded in luring you into putting your hands on me."

"Only on your clothing. Never trust a woman holding a silk noose around your neck."

"Careful, that's workplace violence."

Claire giggled at the mock outrage in his voice. "That's one point for you. But tonight, I roped you into helping me out."

"True," Helmut said, his voice low. "But I got you alone in the backseat of a car."

Claire's heart thudded in her chest and her breath caught in her throat. She glanced quickly at the Plexiglas partition separating them from the driver, and then out the side window. Helmut shifted in the seat next to her, his knee lightly brushing hers, as if by accident.

Claire took a steadying breath. The backseat of the full-size car suddenly felt like a compact, with his broad shoulders taking up the lion's share of the space. Claire uncrossed her knees and straightened her spine, excruciatingly aware of his warmth and his scent in the small quarters. The light hint of cologne tickled her nose and stole through her, spiraling into a warm fire in her pelvis. She had the sudden urge to wrap herself in that scent, and the strong arms that carried it.

The cab pulled to a halt in front of her building, and Claire grabbed her purse. Before she found her wallet, Helmut tossed a bill through the window in the divider. She opened her door and stepped out into the cooling night air that was, unfortunately, thick with the exhaust from the idling taxi. She walked around behind the cab and stopped short. The black and white checked car pulled away, leaving her gaping at Helmut, standing on the curb.

"I didn't invite you in."

He shrugged. "I'll just walk you to your door. My mother would skin me alive if I left a woman alone on a dark city street."

Claire glanced up and down her block, full of hulking warehouses. Some buildings, like hers, were being converted into loft apartments. The neighborhood was considered trendy by the few, transitional by the many. She walked past him, and headed for the brick archway that covered the street-side door. She could feel Helmut following her steps.

The door opened before Claire reached it, and her two downstairs neighbors walked out.

"Thanks." She smiled, and went inside. Helmut followed, still just behind.

She passed the elevators and took the wide wooden stairs at a slight jog up to the third floor. Claire stopped to extract her keys from the bottom of her purse, and Helmut braced one arm against the wall beside her, his breathing much calmer than hers.

"You lead a merry chase," he said.

"A little exercise never hurt anyone."

She met Helmut's gaze in the dimly lit hallway. In his darkened eyes, she recognized the same burning attraction she'd been flirting with all evening, but he held something back.

Claire's fingers closed on her keys, and she tried to pull them out of the bag, but they snagged on the strap and tumbled from her grasp.

Almost before they hit the concrete floor, Helmut was on his knees at Claire's feet, retrieving them. He stood slowly, his body a mere breath from hers. Though he didn't so much as brush her clothing, her breasts tingled at the heat radiating from his chest. If her heart beat any harder, it would have smacked him in the face.

This close, Claire could see a faint touch of stubble darkening his squared jaw, her eyes level with his Adam's apple, above the finely tailored dress shirt that fit closely to firmly muscled shoulders. He wore no tie, and the top button was undone, showing a small hint of tanned, supple skin. Claire's knees went weak at the thought of unbuttoning that shirt and running her fingers across his chest.

She watched, dazed, as he reached his left arm around her, his sleeve brushing her waist, and fit her door key into the lock. He leaned his head down as he reached around her, until they stood almost cheek to cheek. Claire closed her eyes as she felt his warm breath tickling her neck, her ear.

It had been a long time since any man had seduced her so subtly. It had been a long time since any man had seduced her at all. After Frank, she had promised herself to avoid work-related relationships, and she had no time to meet men anywhere else. But from what she knew of Helmut, he didn't do relationships. Heartbreaker. Cold-hearted snake. Hot-blooded man. One who might leave her bed and not dog her steps for years. That didn't sound bad.

With a click, he turned the knob and pushed the massive wood door open.

"I will see you tomorrow," he whispered, the baritone of his voice sending shivers down her spine.

Claire's eyes flew open as he stepped away and cool air replaced the radiating heat of his body. She slumped against her open doorway and watched dumbly as he retreated back down the stairs.

Helmut slid into the hard plastic seat of the mostly empty red-line train. With a squeal, the subway car pulled out of the station, beginning the twenty-some minute trip to his condo. A cab would go faster, but he was in no rush.

He had needed the brisk walk from Claire's apartment to cool his heated blood. In the harsh light of the train, he had to stop dwelling on the night's events or he would embarrass himself.

She had wanted him to kiss her. He didn't miss the turned up lips or her expectant intake of breath. He could be there now, inside that artist's loft of an apartment, her long legs wrapped around him. Maybe she would ride him, long blond hair brushing his face, surrounding him with the scent of sweet coconut and tropical orchids.

Helmut eased off his sports jacket and draped it casually across his lap, disguising a rock hard erection.

He could turn around and head back now, maybe pick up a bottle of champagne at the corner liquor store. His bet would be won. Tomorrow at the office could be awkward, but most of the executive team would be leaving next Tuesday for the Paris Air Show. By the time Claire returned from France, there would be nothing but frosty politeness between them. That's how these things usually went.

Claire wasn't one of his usual flings. She had twice the intelligence and three times the wit of any of the women he'd dated over the past decade. She kept him on his toes with her sharp questions about his department, about their competitors, the marketplace.

She had held her own this morning in a short interview with Aviation Weekly. He and two of the VP's had been in the room, ready to jump to her aid if the interviewer had asked a question over her head. He should have known James' daughter wouldn't need anyone's help to do her job. She had serious potential as a CEO.

She had serious potential for a hot interlude.

He knew already it would take more than one night for him to get enough of her. Maybe he could take her for a weekend getaway somewhere. Somewhere romantic. Somewhere like Paris. Helmut chuckled to himself, drawing a few curious glances from the other passengers.

Claire and a handful of the other executives had a week of product demonstrations, press interviews, and meetings with potential customers lined up at the huge trade show. He himself had an invitation to speak on a panel, and offers for coffees, lunches, and two separate golf outings with some of his counterparts from other companies. There would be plenty of time to spend at Claire's side as her advisor by day, and to romance her by evening. He would have Betty make the arrangements in the morning.

And if all went well, he would be extending his stay by a couple of sweet, hot days.

Chapter 5

Steph set a mug of coffee in front of Claire.

Claire flashed her assistant a smile and wrapped her fingers around the cup, warming her fingers on the hot porcelain for a moment before lifting it to her lips for a delicate sip. If the liquid weren't just shy of boiling, she would be gulping it.

She had not slept well last night after Helmut left her at her door. Logically, she knew she was exhausted, but her blood had refused to cool.

She should have invited him in.

Her condo was cold. And lonely. She normally took comfort in the clean, uncluttered loft space. Twelve foot ceilings, full-height windows with a killer view of downtown, polished concrete floors and sleek granite countertops. Home had never looked so hard and unfeeling.

Since she and Frank had split, she'd had only one relationship. If you could call three dates and one night of mediocre sex a relationship. Frank was a lying, manipulative asshole, but his arms had been warm and the sex good. When he wasn't secretly screwing one of the interns. It had taken a few of his affairs — and the accompanying bedroom dry spells — before Claire caught on to his philandering.

In the months after the split, she would dream about faceless lovers, who brought her to the edge of climax and left her hanging. In one recurring dream, the man would transform into a giant bird and fly away, leaving her trapped on the edge of a cliff, quivering with need and terrified of falling to her death. By day, Frank's self-serving attitude cooled off any lingering thoughts of a reconciliation.

Last night when she closed her eyes, it was Helmut's stubble-roughened square-cut jaw that hovered just out of reach.

This morning, Helmut sat at the far end of the conference table, looking cool and collected as he watched the video conferencing screen, without a hint of a dark shadow beneath his eyes. And he was infuriatingly friendly this morning. Friendly like a coworker, not friendly like a man who wanted to see her naked. Why couldn't the man have the decency to look a little tortured, or at least interested?

He looked up and caught her gaze, and Claire saw the tiniest gleam in his eyes. A thrill shot through her. But then he just nodded politely and looked back at the video screen where the VP of their European division was giving his report.

"Your investment strategy sounds risky," Gene, her Chief Operating Officer, said. "Do we really want to put all of our eggs in with the European Union?"

Claire snapped her focus back to the debate at the table, over a proposed expansion plan.

"Non, non, Gene," the VP said in her heavily accented English. "This is the future. If we get our, how do you say, leg caught in the door now, then we shall benefit greatly from the expanding of the European Union."

Claire glanced around the table. "What does everyone else think?"

"I think Marie is right. Now is the time. We should go for it." Helmut's voice washed down Claire's spine, and she swallowed a sigh of pleasure at the sound.

"Smack dab in the middle of our new military venture?" Gene asked. "We'd be spreading our resources too thin. I say we wait until the defense division has proven itself before we jump into any more new territory."

"Are you always a risk-taker, Helmut?" Claire asked.

Helmut cracked a lopsided grin and shrugged. A round of chuckles from the board answered the question for him.

"Because Gene is correct that we already have our fingers in quite a few pies," she continued.

"Nothing ventured, nothing gained." Their gazes locked across the table, and Claire recognized a challenge in his eyes that had nothing to do with Europe.

"I agree the potential gains are tempting. But are you willing to risk your job?"

"That's the beauty of it. It's not my job I'm risking, Claire. It's yours."

Claire raised one eyebrow. "That's where you're wrong, Helmut. You risk all of our jobs," she said softly and turned back toward the teleconference camera.

"Marie, I agree that the idea might be worthwhile, but I want to see more detail. Since speed is of the essence, you can give me a full report in person next Wednesday in Paris."

"Oui, madame," Marie said. "In Paris."

"There is a problem with Paris." Betty peered over the rims of her reading glasses at Helmut.

He grinned. "I can survive a week in a city without a baseball team."

"My, you're in a good humor this morning." Her tone was crisp, but Helmut caught the quirk of the older lady's lips. "It isn't your entertainment that concerns me."

Helmut picked up one of the small twisted nail puzzles she kept on her desk and began turning it over in his fingers. "What is it?"

"Did you see the memo this morning about the corporate credit cards?"

"I skimmed it." Someone in human resources had lost their laptop, which held a personnel database with employee names, addresses, and corporate card numbers. It was an identity thief's wet dream. "HR needs to start encrypting all their data. That's been standard operating procedure for Finance for years now."

"Yes, I'm sure they're working on it. In the meantime, your personal information was in that database, and the credit company has already suspended all of those cards, just in case. They're issuing us new ones, but the numbers won't be available until Monday at the earliest."

Helmut had a feeling he knew where this discussion was heading. "We can't cancel the whole industry-wide Air Show next week for a batch of stolen cards."

"Of course not. I have your plane tickets on hold with the travel agent for another hour. It's the last first-class ticket out of Chicago leaving any time before next Friday. Shall I use your personal card for the reservation?"

Helmut twisted the nails and pulled. The pair remained annoyingly attached. "No problem. What about the hotel?"

"Same."

He set the puzzle back in its place. "Fine. What's the rest of my day look like?"

"The finance all-hands meeting starts in twenty minutes. You have a lunch appointment with Goldman Sachs, a conference call this afternoon, quarterly statements to review, and your racquetball league at four-thirty." Betty raised one eyebrow. "Would you like me to show you the trick to those nail puzzles?"

"Nah," Helmut said. "I'll figure them out one of these days."

"If you say so."

Claire wrapped a thin towel around her torso, her panties, and the jogging bra she'd worn for her afternoon run on the treadmill. She cracked the door of the private changing room and glanced down the short hall. All clear.

The gym, situated in the basement of the thirty-story office building that housed Sheffield & Fox's corporate headquarters, had been built as an executive-only workout facility back in the sixties. Back when "executive" meant "all-male."

The facility was top-notch. Except for the locker rooms. Obviously limited for space, the gym had a handful of private dressing rooms, only two with showers, all non-gendered. And there was only a single steam room. She preferred to steam in the nude, but wasn't quite up to crossing the hall with just a towel on. Not with other employees around. Next time she'd pack a swimsuit.

Her shower shoes flopped on the linoleum as she scampered across the hall to the shiny stainless steel door. Claire heaved it open and shimmied inside, closing it quickly behind her. She took a deep breath, filling her lungs with the hot steam. With a sigh of pleasure, she sank down on the nearest bench, and relaxed backward against the wall.

"Who's there?"

Claire jumped at the voice. In one corner, Helmut's head swirled into view through the mist. Dark hair clung to his head, curling and damp. She could just make out his neck and the hint of more dark curls at the top of his obviously bare chest.

"You scared me," she said lamely, quickly hopping to her feet, clasping her towel tightly above her breasts. "I didn't see anyone in here."

"Sorry. I was starting to doze. Don't go on my account."

Claire hesitated.

"If you want privacy, I can leave," he offered. The mist cleared temporarily and she caught a glimpse of navy blue workout shorts below tanned and rippling abs.

Claire gave herself a mental shake. They were both adults. Mostly-dressed adults. She sat stiffly and focused on arranging the folds of her towel to cover as much of her bare hips as she could.

"I didn't see you in the gym. Did you just come for a steam?" she asked to fill the awkward silence.

"I was in the racquetball courts. You?" His voice was clearing, sounding more awake.

"Treadmill," she answered.

The silence stretched out between them again. Claire sat back and tried to close her eyes. Her traitorous mind called up a picture of his bare chest. Irritably, she tucked one leg up under her, and swung the other foot, flip-flop dangling from one toe.

"It's usually pretty quiet in here on a Friday after work," Helmut said.

"I imagine everyone has somewhere more exciting to go than to the gym." The heat was beginning to take effect. She could feel some of the tension melting out of her shoulders.

"I like the quiet."

"Me, too. I get some of my best thinking done when I'm running." Claire shifted again, wondering if that was a hint that he wanted her to leave. Too late now if he did. Her legs felt like lead, and she had no intention of rising for at least ten more minutes.

Claire's calves were tight, and she wanted to massage them, but there was no way to do it without dropping the towel. She settled for stretching first one leg out in front of her, and twirling her foot around, alternately stretching and flexing the tight muscles. She untucked her other foot from under her knee. Her flip-flop flew off and skidded across the floor, bumping into Helmut's big toe.

Chapter 6

Helmut picked up the shoe and turned it over in his fingers. The hot pink and yellow floral foam looked entirely too girlish for the woman sitting across from him.

Claire's towel hid far too much, yet revealed far too much, for his comfort. Seated, she was bare to almost the apex of her sleekly muscled thighs. Just below toned shoulders, the scraggly white terry cloth strained over her rounded breasts and skimmed the slim waistline and curve of her hip.

Her cheeks flushed, damp with exertion and steam, and she looked both invigorated and sated, as if she had spent the past hour making love instead of running on a treadmill.

His cock was already half-aroused, straining against his shorts under the towel in his lap. Helmut drew a steadying breath. He didn't think about what he was about to do. He swept the towel aside, and knelt in front of Claire.

"May I?" he said, indicating her foot.

Claire's bright blue eyes glowed luminously against her warm pink cheeks, and her tongue peeked out to discretely lick her lips. Slowly she inclined her head.

Helmut gingerly picked up her bare right foot, noting the pink nail polish and slender toes. The foot looked dainty and pale against his sun-darkened hands. He traced the arch and around the back of her heel. He heard the faint sound of the intake of her breath as she realized that he wasn't just replacing the shoe.

But she didn't pull away.

Helmut slid one hand up the back of her calf to the soft spot behind her knee. Gently, he lifted her foot to his mouth and pressed a light kiss to the bone on the inside of her ankle. She exhaled, slowly.

Helmut trailed his lips upward toward her knee. He kissed her again, savoring the salty sweetness of her skin with his tongue. He glanced upwards. Her eyes blazed into his, the pupils dilated and her lips parted in a soft O.

The heavy steam of the room filled his lungs as he inhaled slowly, languidly. Raggedly. The heat slowed each of his movements into a leisurely exploration of her satiny skin. The pace suited him perfectly. He wanted to savor her taste. To savor her.

He kissed the pulsing vein throbbing on the inside of her knee again, and slid his hand up the outside of her thigh to her hip. He hesitated a moment at the edge of her towel. Allowed her a moment to tell him to stop. Hoped like hell she wouldn't.

Helmut's cock strained against his shorts, and he felt the pounding of his blood rushing through his veins.

Claire closed her eyes and tilted her head back a tiny notch.

Helmut's hand slid up and under her towel along her hip until it found the thin band of fabric and elastic. He toyed with that spot, under the jut of her hipbone, and kissed the inside of her thigh. She shivered and relaxed her leg wider.

Helmut closed his eyes, inhaling the musky scent of her arousal mixed with the sweet, tropical scent of her skin. His fingers trembled at the edge of her panties. Slow. Steady. Don't rush this. Don't ruin this.

With both hands, he reached inside her towel up along the sides of her waist, over the supple skin. Kneeling between her legs, he slowly opened the towel. She let it go and raised her hands and then lowered them, as if she didn't know where to put them.

Helmut smiled at the sight of her purple and black sports bra and sensible white bikini panties. He cupped breasts lightly with his thumbs and lowered his mouth to the confining fabric.

Claire gasped audibly as he closed his mouth over one peak, and the nipple tightened. He kissed and sucked the other breast, teasing the skin around the bottom of the bra band with his fingers.

"Helmut." Claire threaded her fingers into his sweat-slickened hair. "This is not a good idea."

"Do you want me to stop?" He waited, her breast heavy in his palm, his thumb poised on one straining nipple. He rubbed the pad over the taut peak lightly.

She drew a ragged breath and arched her back, pressing against his hands. "No, don't stop."

Helmut's lips left her breasts and he forged a trail of hot kisses down her ribcage to her belly button. He pressed his thumbs up and under the taut fabric of her bra and found hot, sensitive skin. She moaned. His cock throbbed in reply, full and impatient. It would have to wait.

He knew how this encounter would end. Or rather, how it would not end for him. He hadn't walked into the steam room expecting to find himself in this position. He had no condom. It was a cooling thought. Barely.

He bent to kiss her sex through the silky white fabric of her panties. He gently nibbled her clit with his teeth, and she writhed and arched her hips up against his mouth.

He grasped her hips with his fingers and raised them up, and then slid down her panties. The hair between her legs was a deep golden yellow, a few shades darker than her hair. She was definitely a natural blond. He shifted his position to remove the scrap of fabric from her ankles. She parted her legs, willingly allowing him access.

"Please," she whispered.

Helmut felt the first drops of his own fluids at the tip of his penis, and clamped down hard on the sensation. Ladies first. His thighs quavered as he bent between her legs, and spread her folds with his fingers.

Claire writhed and moaned as he slipped one finger across her wet opening. He slid it inside as he rubbed the swollen bud of her clit with his thumb. She arched and rubbed against him, urging his fingers in further, against the hard bundle of nerves inside.

She was close. Helmut wanted to be inside her, to feel her tighten around his cock, to slide into her folds and to bury his face in the long blond hair. He wanted her to come for him.

He bent his head and took her clit into his mouth, sucking and licking the sensitive bud with his tongue. At the same time, he slid a second finger inside her and worked them, sliding them in and out. He heard her gasp, and moan, and her fingers clutched his hair.

"Helmut."

His name on her lips was nearly his own undoing as he felt her tighten around his fingers. He felt the rush of her fluids, and sucked her again. She shifted on his fingers, pumping up and down and tightened around him again and again.

When she stilled, he raised his lips and kissed the inside of her thigh. She protested softly as he removed his fingers from her sex, and gently set her hips down on the bench.

"That was...you didn't..." she began.

Helmut looked into those angelic blue eyes, gazing at him with a rapturous expression. Despite his own painfully throbbing erection, he felt a burst of manly pride.

A clamor of voices in the hallway shocked him into awareness.

"We aren't alone." He carefully wrapped her back in her towel, and reluctantly stood up. His cock was hard at attention beneath his shorts, but there was no hope for it. He grabbed for his towel and held it limply in one hand.

"I'll head out first. Wait a few minutes. Or do you want me to knock when the coast is clear?"

Claire reached for the underwear that had been dropped on the floor and balled them in one fist. She straightened. "I'll manage."

Helmut turned toward the door. He recognized the timber of men's voices. Could be Ben, or some of the other racquetball players, fresh from their showers. Thank God none of them had felt like a steam after the match.

"Helmut?"

He looked over his shoulder. Claire had smoothed her hair back from her face. This time, he could take credit for the flush in her cheeks and the sparkle in her eyes. "Yes?"

"Shall we finish this at my place?"

"Absolutely."

Chapter 7

"You're where?" Helmut practically shouted into the phone. The connection cut out again and his palms went frigid.

"--eoria," came Kelsie's voice.

"Peoria? What the hell are you doing in Peoria?" Helmut leaned one balled fist on the kitchen counter in front of him. "I thought Mom said you were spending the week in New York."

"My phone's about to die. Can you come get me? Please? I'll explain when you get here. I'm in the Denny's on University just off 74."

"Yeah. I'm on my way."

Helmut clicked off his cell phone and stared at the faint blue screen. Assuming his baby sister was safe and sound when he got to Peoria, he was going to strangle her.

Helmut buzzed the doorman to his condo building and requested that the valet bring his car up from the underground garage. The drive to Peoria would take him three hours at least. Thankfully it was well past rush hour, or he would be fighting the parking lot that was I-55 as downtown Chicago emptied for the weekend.

Helmut glanced down at the bouquet of exquisite red roses, still wrapped in a generous sheaf of green florist paper. He hunted through the numbers in his cell phone. Nada.

Helmut swore under his breath as he dialed Betty.

"Hello?" She sounded distracted, and Helmut thought he heard the friendly chatter of voices in the background.

"Betty, it's Helmut. I'm very sorry to call you at home."

"That's OK. What do you need?"

"Do you have Claire's cell phone number? Or a land line?"

He heard the background noise on Betty's end grow louder and then go silent, as if she'd shut a door.

"Claire? You mean Sheffield?"

"Yes." Helmut walked to his coat closet and pulled out his old leather jacket.

"I can pull it up on my laptop computer. Darned fancy technology. This is going to take me a few minutes to power up. Are you in the office? Can I call you back?" Helmut heard the rustling of papers.

"I'm at home. Leaving it actually. Call my cell."

"Sure. What's going on?"

"I, uh, was supposed to go over, uh, something with her tonight. But I've got a family emergency."

"Did something happen to your mom?" she asked, the pitch of her voice rising. Helmut could picture the concern on her face. Betty had only met his mother once or twice over the years, but the two women got along well.

"No, no. It's Kelsie." He heard the faint chime of the laptop powering on.

"Your sister? You're going to Florida? Do I need to rearrange your schedule for Monday?"

"Calm down, Betty. Kelsie's fine. She's just stranded in Peoria. And no, I don't know how that happened. But I intend to find out in a few hours."

"Some crazy college stunt, no doubt," she said. "I found the number. Are you ready?"

Helmut grabbed the first envelope off a stack of mail and hurriedly scribbled down the digits as she read them off. "Thanks, Betty. Again, I'm sorry to interrupt you."

"I know you are, Helmut. Go take care of your sister, and I'll see you at the baseball game tomorrow afternoon."

The Cubs game. He had almost forgotten. He had arranged for his department to use the company box for the Cubs-Cards game. "About that. Any chance that there's an extra ticket? In case I have company for the weekend."

Betty chuckled. "I'll see what I can do. Safe driving."

Helmut clicked off his phone and headed out the door to the elevator. As he rode down the twenty-three floors to street level, he dialed Claire's number. It went straight to voice mail.

Helmut frowned into the phone as the doorman handed him his car keys.

"Claire, it's Helmut. I hate to cancel on you like this, but something came up. I will make it up to you as soon as I can."

He slid behind the driver's seat of his BMW, slamming the door shut at the same time he clicked off the phone.

The caustic mix of anger, frustration, and fear had faded into weariness by the time he pushed open the glass door of the little restaurant. The monotonous landscape of rural Illinois had droned the fight out of him.

He immediately spotted the familiar petite brunette, sitting in a corner booth with her legs stretched out before her, reading a paperback book. He slid into the opposite end of the booth and signaled for the waitress. And Kelsie pounced.

"You're here!" She threw her arms around him and buried her head in his chest.

Helmut gave her a squeeze and carefully set her away from him. Her eyes were puffy and red and she exhaled a shuddering breath. Clad in a pair of faded, low-hipped jeans and a gray hoodie with her long hair pulled back into a simple ponytail, she looked far younger than her twenty-one years.

"What happened, kiddo?" he asked.

"We were on our way to Iowa City, to visit some friends — "

"We who?" Helmut demanded.

Kelsie's cheeks reddened and she twirled the straw in a half-empty soda glass. "It doesn't matter. I'm never seeing him again."

"Kelsie."

She looked back up at him, with the same stubborn set to her chin that she used to have when she'd get in trouble as a kid. "His name is Chris. We've been dating for a couple of weeks, and we both have friends at Iowa State, so we decided to take a road trip. I told Mom I was headed up to Laura's in New York. I knew she'd freak if she found out I was going on a trip with a guy. She treats me like I'm fifteen, or something."

Helmut raised an eyebrow. "Go on."

"Anyway, just past Indianapolis, he got a phone call from some other girl. I asked who it was, and he started on some rant about how he'd never agreed to date me exclusively."

"You got in a fight, so he dropped you on the side of the road?" Beneath the table, Helmut clenched is hands into fists. His sister was impulsive, and as the baby of the family, more than a little spoiled. But she was still his sister. And if this Chris-guy had been standing nearby, Helmut would have decked him.

Her pink cheeks deepened to a bright crimson. "No, he didn't kick me out. We didn't talk at all the last hour in the car. When he stopped for gas across the street, I got out and walked away."

Helmut took a deep breath and slowly exhaled, willing his fists to unclench. Impulsive, spoiled, *and* willful.

"Can I get you something?" the waitress asked.

"The check," Kelsie said.

"Coffee. Black," Helmut said.

"I've been sitting here for three and a half hours," Kelsie said. "Can't we go?"

"I've been up since five this morning, worked all day, and played an hour and a half of racquetball. And I've been driving for three and a half hours." Not to mention Claire and the steam room. "Unless you're willing to take the wheel, I need caffeine."

"Oh. Right. Fancy sports car with the fancy stick shift." She picked up her ponytail with one hand and began twirling the ends around her fingers. "Rob offered to teach me, you know."

Helmut raised an eyebrow. "To teach you what?"

"To drive a stick, of course. Sometime when he's home."

He sighed. Their brother hadn't been home in years. He was too busy with his research on Brazilian tree frogs to come home and teach his baby sister how to drive a stick shift. Or to call their mother. "Do you hear from him much, Kelsie?"

"An email here and there. He's on Facebook, too. I actually chatted with him for a few minutes last month when he was in Sao Paolo." She cocked her head to one side. "Haven't you guys made up yet?"

The waitress arrived and deposited a chipped ceramic mug and a pot of coffee on the table in front of Helmut, and he busied himself adding cream and sugar. He raised the mug to his lips and inhaled the steam. It was way too hot to sip. Unfortunately.

"I take it that's a 'no'?" she asked.

Helmut sighed and set the cup back down. He ran one hand through his hair, smoothing the lock by his forehead that was so often out of place. "He's never called, no."

"Maybe you should be the big brother here, Helmut, and call first. Maybe if he thought he was welcome, he might come back to the States once in a while."

And maybe Brazilian tree frogs would sprout feathers. "Look, Kelsie, I appreciate your concern but this isn't any of your business."

"But—"

"With all due respect, butt out. Rob's a big boy. If he wants to live his life in the Amazon jungle, it's his decision. I'm not going to try and talk him out of it. And don't—"

She opened her mouth to protest again.

He held up his hand to cut her off but deliberately softened his voice. "Let it go, please."

She crossed her arms over her chest and slunk backwards into the booth seat, her pose more protesting than defeated.

Helmut took a gulp of his rapidly cooling coffee. It was too strong and tasted bitter, even with the additions. He understood his sister's frustration. He wanted Rob home as much as Kelsie and Mom did. But after their father died ten years ago, he and Rob had a major blowup. He had accused his younger brother of skipping on family responsibilities, and his brother had accused Helmut of having a stick up his ass, and a teenaged Kelsie had cried through the whole argument. And then, in the thick of it, Rob had just left. Turned and walked out.

At least his younger brother was starting to talk to Kelsie again. Helmut drained his cup. At least his younger brother was talking to someone again.

"Helmut?"

"Yes, Kelsie?"

"Thanks, big brother. For coming to pick me up. I am glad you're here." Her voice was soft and shy, and Helmut spared her a glance out of the corner of his eye. She was looking at him with her wide brown eyes and a hopeful vulnerability that melted just a tiny corner of his heart.

Kelsie was almost seventeen years younger than he was. And she'd had him wrapped around her little finger since the day she'd first learned to smile. If she was spoiled, it was because she was so easy to spoil. His lips quirked into a half grin, and he slid one arm around her slim shoulders.

"That's what family's for, kiddo," he said, and gave her a squeeze.

Chapter 8

"Your friend Helmut keeps himself busy."

Claire clenched her teeth as the smug undertone of Frank's nasal voice grated along her last nerve.

"That is his name, right? Helmut? You two were very chummy at the concert."

The late May afternoon was sunny, it was a perfect seventy-five degrees, and the Cubs were actually favored to win over the Cards. Claire had been looking forward to the outing with the girls for three months. The four friends—Claire, Steph, Jen, and Alicia—had been friends since college, and shared an apartment for two crazy, party-filled years after graduation. Now they all had busy careers that sent them to the far ends of the country. Get-togethers like this were too precious to waste.

"Why is he here?" she whispered to Steph.

"Frank or Helmut?"

"Frank," she ground out.

"Alice and her brother, Doug, went together on tickets, to qualify for the group rate. You two weren't so, well, distant last fall when we were planning this. Just ignore him, Claire,"

Steph said. Doug and Frank had been frat brothers and Claire had forgotten all about Alice's brother.

"No, this has got to stop. Now." Claire turned around in her seat, and whipped the blue and white baseball cap off her head.

"What? I'm just making small talk." Frank shrugged.

"Out with it, Frank. What's got you gloating this morning?"

"Oh, it's nothing. I had thought that you and the guy you were with at the concert were together. That's all."

Claire seethed. Frank's guess was far too close to the truth. But after last night, it was not a subject she cared to argue about. Least of all with her slimy ex. "We're just coworkers, Frank."

"Then you wouldn't be upset to see him with the hottie up in that skybox." Frank took a swig of his beer and sat back, feigning boredom. Claire saw the look he snuck under lowered lashes, daring her to look.

Claire glanced up toward S&F's box, cursing Frank under her breath. She had wanted to use it for today's game instead of their general admission seats, but it was already spoken for. One of the other departments had reserved the box for the day.

"Finance is having an outing here today," Steph said.

Claire whipped back around to her friend. "Quit that."

"What?" Steph asked.

"Reading my mind. It's eerie."

"You're not that hard to read, girlfriend." Steph grinned. "And it's my job to keep track of all of the little details so you can focus on corporate strategy and all that bullshit."

Claire chanced another glance upwards toward the box. She saw a curvy brunette leaning forward over the railing, but she couldn't make out her face. She didn't remember a young brunette in Helmut's office, but everyone looked different in jeans and baseball hats than they did in skirts and suits.

Not that she cared. She was absolutely not jealous. Not at all. Frank was trying to rile her, and it wasn't going to work.

The crowd roared approval as the new first baseman slammed himself into the padded wall to catch a foul ball. Claire cheered and tried to focus on the game.

Helmut had stood her up last night. He left a voicemail, for goodness sake. A voicemail. After the steam room. Maybe the rumors about him were right. Heartbreaker, player, cad. She was just a notch on his belt. A conquest. The fact that he hadn't actually gotten any—she had barely even touched him—wouldn't matter.

"You could pop in if you wanted to. Shake hands, kiss a few babies, do that CEO-goodwill-stuff," Steph suggested.

Claire twirled her hat in one hand. "This is personal time. I haven't seen you girls for months. Well, I haven't seen Jen and Alicia for months. I'm not ditching you to crash someone else's party."

Steph raised one eyebrow and quirked her lips. "I wasn't suggesting you spend the whole game up there. Five minutes should be plenty."

"I don't care who Helmut brought to the baseball game. He could have an entire harem up there, for all the difference it would make to me."

"It's almost the seventh inning stretch. If you go now, you won't get caught in the mad rush for the bathrooms."

One of these days, Steph is going to be wrong about something.

Claire excused herself and squeezed over her friends toward the end of the aisle.

"Good Luck," Alicia called as Claire climbed the stairs. Claire threw a glare over her shoulder at her friends. They had their heads together, and Steph and Jen were giggling like a couple of coeds. In the row behind them, Frank gave her a wink. She took a deep breath and mentally blocked out his smug face.

As she wound her way past the concession stands to the mezzanine, she tried to recall the names and faces of everyone she'd met in Finance this week, something she normally excelled at.

But it was Helmut's gray-green eyes that filled her mind.

Claire paused at the door to the box. The interior of the air-conditioned room had been custom-decorated with navy blue leather seats and small end tables topped in the same granite as the countertop of the built-in wet bar. Framed posters of some of S&F's aircraft were interspersed with Cubs memorabilia on the walls. Claire recognized the baseball bat autographed by Babe Ruth that her father used to display over the fireplace in their den when she was a kid.

Neither Helmut nor the brunette were anywhere to be seen. Claire breathed a quick sigh of relief. The walk up the stairs from the infield had cooled her ire, and she realized how awkward it would be if Helmut were here with a date.

"Ms. Sheffield, what a surprise." Helmut's secretary crossed the room and greeted her warmly. "Helmut forgot to tell me you were coming today."

"Oh, I'm not staying. I am sitting with some friends down by the infield. I just thought I'd stop by and say hello." Claire smiled at the woman. Dressed in khaki capris and a baseball jersey with her long hair loose, Betty looked far different than the tight-laced persona she wore in the office.

"Did he get a hold of you last night? He called me at dinnertime asking for your phone number. It sounded urgent."

Claire startled. He called his secretary? "Um. Yes. He did leave me a message."

"Oh, good. I'm glad things worked out. Well, come in and let me introduce you to a few of the folks you might not have met yet." Betty steered her toward a several family groups, where three or four kids ran circles around the legs of the relaxed, chatting adults.

Claire made small talk with the accounting staff and their families, noting the names of two men and one woman who seemed eager to get face time with their CEO. She'd have Steph check out their records next week. Ambitious workers could be a real asset, or a total pain in the ass, and Steph was an expert at ferreting out the latter.

The eighth inning was about to start when she turned to leave and caught her breath.

Helmut stood at the doorway, a beautiful young woman on his arm. She had thought he looked sexy in tailored slacks, but that was nothing compared to the way a pair of well-worn denim jeans hugged his lean hips and emphasized rock-hard thighs. The T-shirt he wore left his tanned and muscled forearms bare, and Claire's pulse quickened as she remembered those arms tracing up her bare ribcage.

The woman stood on tiptoe and whispered something into Helmut's ear. He chuckled. The bright glow in his eyes as he talked to his date answered all of Claire's doubts. Clearly, they knew each other well. Claire's stomach churned at the thought of all of the sexual fantasies she'd been nurturing the past week. He had been making a fool of her—and of his pretty little girlfriend. She stiffened her spine and raised her chin a notch. The girlfriend was none of Claire's business, and as of now, Helmut was nothing but business to her.

Before she could rip her eyes away from the pair, Helmut spotted her. His eyes darkened as he caught her gaze. Claire's blood boiled at the thinly veiled desire she saw in his eyes. How dare he look at her like that, here, in front of his whole office and his date. She turned sharply on one heel and stalked into the suite's private restroom, closing the door behind her with a snap.

Fool. Wimp. Claire stared at her own image in the bathroom mirror. *You are fearless in the face of television cameras, an auditorium full of stockholders, or a boardroom full of men twice your age. But you are a complete coward when faced with one lone man.*

A speaker in the ceiling announced that the backup pitcher had just taken the mound. Time to get back to her own party. Claire flushed the empty toilet and ran the sink water briefly, for effect, and then lifted her head high and stepped out of the bathroom.

Most of the people had returned to their seats or found spots along the wall of windows overlooking the field, and no one paid any attention to Claire as she slipped out the door and back into the now-empty hallway.

Helmut leaned lazily against the wall, arms crossed over his chest and eyes narrowed at the brunette standing in front of him talking. Claire paused mid-step. There was no way to walk past him without being noticed. Maybe he would ignore her. She schooled her features into a polite mask and started to walk past.

"Claire—"

Claire startled as Helmut's hand touched her sleeve. In his eyes, Claire saw a low simmer that sent a thrill straight to her core. She forced her lips into a polite smile.

"Helmut. You had a nice turnout," she said, indicating the door she just stepped out of.

His lips quirked. "I would like you to meet someone."

Claire gritted her teeth as he put one arm around the woman's shoulder. "Claire Sheffield, this is my sister Kelsie."

Claire's jaw dropped at the word "sister". Was he kidding? The brunette—Kelsie—extended a hand and cocked her head to one side as she studied Claire.

"It's an honor, to meet you in person Mrs. Sheffield. We studied Arachnava last semester in my business strategy course. Your accomplishments there were awesome!"

Claire reeled from the unexpected fan-girl attitude. This girl was Helmut's sister? "Um, great. Are you a, um, student then?"

"I'm majoring in English Lit at the University of Florida, minoring in finance. I'm thinking of going for an MBA. I mean, academia isn't that exciting, and there aren't a lot of other job opportunities in my field."

Claire smiled and nodded, her mind racing. When Kelsie paused in her rambling monologue to catch her breath, Claire arched one eyebrow at Helmut. "You go to school in Florida. What brings you to Chicago?"

Kelsie crossed her arms across her abdomen. "I, uh, road trip," she mumbled.

Helmut chuckled nervously. "Don't you miss the impulsive college days when you could just drop everything and hit the road for the weekend?"

"Heh. Some days," Claire admitted. The pair were covering up something, but she didn't feel comfortable prying. "Speaking of which, I am here with some of my girlfriends. I should get back before they send out a scouting party. It was nice to meet you, Kelsie. Have a nice weekend, Helmut."

Claire shook Kelsie's hand and turned to leave.

"A word before you go?" asked Helmut. "Kelsie, I'll be back in a minute."

Helmut waited for Kelsie to roll her eyes and walk back into the suite. Claire's heart fluttered and she fought the urge to twirl her hair like a coed. She shoved her hands into her jeans pockets to keep her fingers from reaching for her ponytail.

"Did you get my message last night?" Helmut asked, his voice low, eyes sparkling.

"Yes," Claire answered carefully. She felt her cheeks flushing as she remembered seeing that same sparkle while he knelt between her knees in the steam room. She dropped her gaze from Helmut's eyes. Big mistake. A few curls of hair peeked out of the neckline of his T-shirt, reminding her of the sight of his bare chest. Luckily her fingers were safely ensconced in her pockets or she might have reached out to touch that broad expanse of muscle.

He shifted his stance, and Claire felt a little tinge of satisfaction at putting him in awkward spot. "Is yesterday's invitation still open?" he asked.

The sound of a door opening down the hall startled Claire. A man emerged from one of the other boxes, talking loudly on his cell phone. Horror dawned at her own reaction. She had been on the verge of saying "yes." "I don't know if it's such a good idea..."

A shadow passed over Helmut's eyes, but was quickly replaced by his customary twinkle. "What happens on the weekend," he said with a lazy smile, "doesn't have to come to the office on Monday."

Claire inhaled deeply. Another big mistake. The spicy scent of Helmut's cologne filled her nostrils and spread through her veins like whiskey. "I'm busy tonight," she said.

"Understood." Helmut's gaze raked down her figure, and Claire felt her nipples hardening in response.

"Have a nice night, Claire," he said softly, his voice sliding over her heated body like velvet. He turned and walked slowly back to the suite door.

"I might be home tomorrow." Her voice was a whisper. Surely too quiet for him to hear.

He paused at the door and glanced back. Claire spun on her heel, startled to have been caught watching him walk away. But she didn't miss the slight nod of his head before she fled the hall.

Chapter 9

Claire set her coffee cup onto the polished granite kitchen countertop with a hard clank. She had no idea who would buzz her apartment's intercom at this ungodly hour of — well, damn, was it ten-thirty in the morning already?

She pressed the intercom button. "Who's there?"

Her voice sounded dry and crackled from the second hand smoke of the martini bar where she and the girls had ended their evening last night. This morning. Whatever.

The intercom sounded just slightly more clear than a kindergartener with a tin can and a string, and she buzzed her mystery guest up. Three inches of solid oak in her loft's front door could keep any violent intruder at bay long enough to call the cops.

Claire smoothed one hand through her long, thick hair and glanced around for her glasses. She couldn't remember if she'd put them on when she got out of bed and the tortoise shell framed blended all too well with the variegated browns and tans of her counters. She had trained herself to make coffee while semi-conscious and semi-blind back in college.

She headed to the door when she heard the knock, wincing as her bare feet left the warm wood of the kitchen and touched the frigid concrete of the entry. Claire peered through the peephole and pulled back, blinking away the morning sleep fog.

Surely that wasn't...

She peered again, squinting through the tiny glass circle.

It was.

Claire clutched the edges of her fluffy pink robe together over her pounding heart. She glanced down at herself. She was literally bedraggled, wearing pajamas and her hair slightly wild from sleep. She had barely removed her makeup and brushed her teeth before crawling between the sheets and crashing. Quickly, she smoothed down her hair and tucked the sides behind her ears. She could ignore him and hope he went away.

He knocked again.

From what she knew of Helmut, he wasn't the type to back away from something he wanted. And clearly he wanted her. The thought sent a shiver of desire down her spine.

Hell, he'd already seen her in workout clothes. And out of workout clothes.

Claire yanked the massive door open, and jumped back as a bouquet of roses nearly smacked her in the nose.

"Sorry," said Helmut. "Didn't mean to scare you."

The roses were close enough for her to make out their details. They were wide open, and the stems were wrapped with...paper towels?

She glanced up at Helmut questioningly.

"They were fresh Friday night," he said with a half-smile. "Kelsie's had them in a bowl of ice water for the past two days. I think she felt bad about interrupting my night out and was hoping she could salvage the flowers."

"Oh," said Claire, as she accepted the bundle. "Um, thank you. I think. Maybe I should look for a vase?"

She turned and started to walk back to the kitchen, and realized that Helmut wasn't following. When she looked back, he was still standing in the doorway. She couldn't quite see his facial features, but he had one hand propped in the doorway, and was poised just outside the threshold. Something about his body language looked hesitant. It wasn't an emotion she associated with the bold, laughing executive she'd worked with all week.

"Would you like to come in? I just made coffee."

"Coffee would be great."

Claire was sure the glow of his face was the blur of a wide grin.

His footsteps behind her were unhurried as she led the way back to her kitchen. She took care of the flowers and pulled a second mug off of the small wooden rack that set next to the small, 4-cup coffee maker. She gave another furtive glance around for the missing glasses, and sighed in defeat as she poured him a cup.

"I don't have cream, but there might be some milk in the fridge. I don't know about sugar." Claire held out the mug.

Helmut crossed the kitchen with deliberate strides. He stepped close and his face swam into view, his eyes glowing. The scent of steaming coffee mixed with the spicy undertones of his cologne. Desire pooled in Claire's abdomen. She was suddenly too aware of the ridiculous robe she wore, and of how unprepared she felt to have a man in her kitchen. Especially this man.

The brush of his fingers sent a thrill through Claire's nervous system as Helmut gently took the cup out of her hands. He stood close. So close that the tips of his loafers whispered against her bare toes and the heat from his body warmed the exposed skin of her chest.

Claire drew in a breath, and let her gaze travel upwards from his long, tanned fingers, over the light cream-colored sweater that stretched across his toned shoulders. The fabric looked soft and luxe, and she had a silly urge to rub her cheek against it to see if it felt as cozy and inviting as it looked. His chest rose and fell in time with her own. Was he as nervous as she felt?

Without a sip, Helmut set the coffee mug down on the counter beside him.

Claire dragged her gaze back to his eyes, and her breath caught in her throat. Nervousness was the farthest thing from his eyes. Her core turned to molten lead.

She had never seen green fire until now. She gulped.

"I want you to know that I'm not looking for anything complicated right now," she said with a whisper.

"No?" He stepped a hair closer. Her nipples stood erect, straining toward the heat of his body.

"I've done complicated. And an office romance. A complicated office romance. I don't need another one of those." She licked her lips nervously.

Helmut took another small step closer. "You want something simple?"

She nodded. And gulped as desire flooded her veins and made her heartbeat erratic.

"Simple is good."

Then his lips caught hers and erased all traces of logic from her brain. He kissed her hard and hungry, and she parted her lips and returned the kiss. Claire ran her hands up that sexy sweater, pressing her fingers against the hard muscles underneath. He grasped her waist and pulled her against him, almost roughly, and Claire grasped two fistfuls of the knit fabric to keep from losing her balance.

He pivoted and pinned her with the hard length of his body against the countertop, the edge digging into the backs of her buttocks. Claire's breasts were flattened against his chest, straining against the fluff of the robe, growing heavy.

Helmut's tongue probed Claire's mouth, demanding, and she responded in kind. With a muffled groan, he wedged one leg between hers. His fingers moved impatiently across her waist, finally finding the satiny ties that kept the robe closed. He wrenched his lips from Claire's, trailing hot kisses across her cheek to her earlobe and the hot skin of her neck.

Claire whimpered as he nibbled gently at the spot where her neck met her collarbone. Vaguely, she realized that he still struggled with her robe ties, and she released the death grip she'd held on his sweater to help.

She shoved his fingers aside and quickly located one dangling end of the bow. Helmut's hands cupped her hips, and rounded her bottom. One end of the robe hung open, and Claire quickly reached inside to release the second tie.

Helmut wasted no time slipping the robe from her shoulders, and allowing it to slide to the ground, revealing the thin flannel sleep pants and strappy camisole Claire had slept in. His fingers trailed immediately from her shoulders to her breasts, barely covered by the flimsy cotton fabric.

Claire arched her back as he squeezed her breasts, weighing them and teasing her nipples with his thumbs. He shuffled his feet, kicking the robe out of his way. He pressed one hard thigh between hers again, and Claire eagerly spread hers.

He was kissing her mouth again, licking and sucking her lips while the rock hard bulge of his erection ground against her pelvis. Claire gasped at the friction against her clit through the thin fabric of her pants.

She felt hot all over, and wet. Her panties were soaked with desire and the slow rocking motion of Helmut's hips sent ripples of pleasure washing over her. Claire wanted more of him. Now.

She reached up and under his sweater, yanking up the T-shirt he wore underneath until she found the smooth bare skin of his belly. She traced her fingers around the edge of the waistband of his jeans, reveling in the dip and swells of his muscles. Teasingly, she slipped two fingers down beneath the denim, finding the elastic of his briefs, already bulging around the tip of his cock.

She heard Helmut gasp as her fingers briefly skimmed the head, and she smiled in triumph. Then she slid both palms upward, across his chest and found the tiny buds of his own nipples.

"Tease." His voice was hoarse.

Her exploration of his body cut short as he pulled his hips back and slid a hand down into her panties. Claire moaned as his fingers found her clit and rubbed, then slid farther. He slid one finger, and then two, into her wet folds, his palm still rubbing against her swollen bud. Claire came apart with a shatter of tiny ripples that left her breathless for more.

She unbuttoned his jeans, and cupped the hard bulge of his erection through the heavy cotton of his underwear, reaching underneath to cup his balls.

Claire heard a muffled word spoken against her hair, and Helmut wrenched his hips backward away from her teasing fingers. He slid his hand out of her and pulled her pants off. He lifted her hips up and settled her butt onto the cold granite countertop. She spread her legs wide.

One hand supported her lower back while the other found a condom in his pocket. Claire tugged his jeans down over his hips, and then followed with his briefs while he ripped open the packet with his teeth. From her perch, she couldn't lower them any further, and Helmut was in too much of a hurry to completely remove them.

She took the small latex circle from him, and slowly unrolled it down the hard length of his cock. It stood huge and throbbing among the thicket of dark brown curls of his pubic hair. He gritted his teeth as she rubbed his length.

He positioned himself at her entrance and paused. Claire whimpered, arching her back and rubbing up against his shaft.

He gazed into her eyes. His temples were flushed with exertion and his breath was ragged. Slowly, eyes locked on each other, he pushed himself into her tight opening.

Every centimeter of his languid descent felt like delicious agony to Claire. She could feel the tiny shudders again and grasped his bare, muscled butt, urging him faster, harder. But he continued at the same maddeningly slow pace until she writhed and moaned. And filled every bit of her.

"Please," she whispered, wanting more. Wanting him to move, to slam into her. To claim her completely.

Helmut withdrew almost to the end and slid back into her, teasing. She wriggled her hips, squeezing his cock and rocking her pelvis against him as best she could. She had virtually no leverage to push against, and instead wrapped her legs up and around his waist, urging him deeper. Closer.

She saw the moment his control collapsed. He pumped into her, hard and fast. Claire clung to him, grinding her clit against him on every down thrust, arching her back to maximize friction on her g-spot with every upward pull.

If before she had climaxed with tiny ripples, this one was a full-blown tsunami. She cried out in pleasure as she felt the waves rush over her as thrust again and again. The ripples continued to flow with each thrust until she felt the muscles in his back tighten and he pinned her hips as he came inside her.

Chapter 10

Helmut braced Claire's hips to keep from dropping her backwards onto the cold hard stone as his breathing slowed. He would never look at a kitchen the same way again.

The musky scents of sex and of Claire mingled with the lightly tropical scent that he'd come to associate with her. His face was buried in her hair, and he wondered briefly if it was her shampoo that always reminded him of coconuts.

Claire wriggled her hips lightly and he reluctantly began detangling their bodies. Gently, he settled her bottom more securely on the counter and eased himself out of her. She uncrossed her ankles, loosening that delicious hold she'd had around his waist. He trailed the pads of his hands up the outsides of long, slender thighs to the backsides of her knees as he slowly lowered her legs down.

"Those are the nicest flowers I've ever received," she said with a contented sigh.

Helmut chuckled. "The coffee wasn't bad either. Great kitchen..."

She grinned, and he reached up to tuck a stray lock of her hair back behind one ear. Her temples were flushed a pretty pink and her eyes twinkled a naughty shade of blue.

"Why don't I show you the rest of the place? There are a few more rooms that you might enjoy."

She placed one hand in the middle of Helmut's chest and gave him a playful shove backwards, but he stood his ground. She slid down onto her feet, her body sliding seductively against his during the short descent. He felt his cock stir at the full frontal contact.

"Granite is nice, but it's a little cold." Her voice sounded breathy, and her lips, still swollen from his kisses, were slightly parted. Helmut grinned again and kissed her hard and thoroughly on that plump mouth.

Helmut gripped her bare bottom and pressed her hips hard against his growing erection as her tongue teased and taunted his. With a moan that sounded almost irritated, she wedged her fingers against his chest and gave him another light shove. He released her this time and stepped back.

"Bedroom," she panted. "It's much more comfortable."

Then she bent down in front of him. Helmut gasped as he felt her fingers on the bare flesh of his inner thighs, and then her hands on his hard cock.

"We aren't going anywhere if you keep that up," he said through gritted teeth.

Her hands disappeared along with their beautiful teasing, and she yanked up his pants.

"Better?" she asked with a wicked grin.

"Not really." Helmut's gaze lingered on her lips. A tiny hint pink tongue peeked out to lightly moisten those lips, and he gulped as he imagined that tongue flicking across the head of his penis. "I think you promised a tour?"

His eyes feasted on the sight of her naked ass as she bent over once more to collect her robe and bottoms from the floor. She led the way out of the kitchen, her hips swaying hypnotically in front of him. Helmut felt like a rat following a piper. Right now, he could care less if the stroll ended at a cliff as long as he got his hands on that body of hers again.

The bedroom was separated from the cavernous living space by a series of translucent screens with no door. Claire slipped around behind the nearest one, and he could see the outline of her body silhouetted against the frosted glass. The colors were blurred and he could see only a pink legs beneath the candy red of the little camisole he'd not bothered removing.

She turned, noticing that he still hesitated on the opposite side of the screen wall. She stepped closer, so that he could distinguish the dark shadow of the patch of curls that covered her sex.

He watched, mouth dry, as she slowly lifted her arms and slipped that red camisole up and over her head. The dark pink of her nipples showed clearly, her breasts nearly touching the glass. She crossed her arms to her shoulders, covering her breasts. Helmut began to step away, to come join her.

Her arms dropped. Slowly, seductively, she caressed her own arms until her fingers met at her belly button. And then they slipped upwards, cupping her own breasts. He watched as she ran her thumbs over her nipples, and tilted her head back. Above his own labored breathing, Helmut distinctly heard her soft gasp of pleasure.

One hand left her breast and slid up her neck to her lips. He saw her lick two fingers.

He held his pants with one hand, and his cock throbbed and strained against the cloth, demanding to be freed. But he could not move.

One of her hands squeezed her breast, tweaking the nipple, and the other left her mouth and slid down her sternum. To her belly button. And lower.

Helmut's knees nearly buckled. He fought alternating urges to work his own cock while he watched her pleasure herself, and to join her on the other side of the frosted glass wall.

Her fingers paused just above her clit. She crooked her fingers at him.

It was all the invitation he needed.

He strode purposefully around into the bedroom area, barely breaking his stride as he kicked off shoes, shrugged out of his sweater, and dropped his still un-buckled pants. Claire had perched on the edge of her king-sized bed, covers swept aside.

Her legs were spread wide open in invitation, and her hands moved restlessly across her bare torso. In two strides, he was crawling on top of her as she scooted backwards across the smooth sheets.

"That's my job," he said, capturing her roving hands, and pinning them lightly up above her head.

"I wasn't sure you were coming," she gasped as he nipped gently at her neck.

"Won't be a problem." Helmut trailed kisses across her collarbone. "Trust me."

He took one pert nipple in his mouth and sucked hard. Claire ground her pelvis upward against his erection. Helmut released her hands so that he could freely explore her body, stroking down her sides, cupping her breasts, and lightly rolling her nipples between her fingers until she was panting.

He could feel the moist heat of her sex teasing his tip and he groaned.

"Where are you going?" she panted as he pushed himself up and away. She threaded her hands into his hair and pulled his head down to kiss him hard, her tongue thrusting between his lips. His body felt tight, and he had to mentally clamp down on the urge to bury himself inside her.

"Condom," he said as he wrenched his lips away from hers.

Her eyes, darkened with desire, locked with his, and she nodded. "Nightstand."

She rolled beneath him, and Helmut kissed the curve of her hip as she opened the drawer and rifled through the contents. Her backside was nearly facing him and he kissed her just above the swell of her bottom, and slipped one finger down and between her legs into her hot, wet opening.

Claire moaned and arched her hips upwards against the pressure of his fingertips, and he thrust them inside her as she writhed against him. But after a moment, she regained control and freed herself from his hand.

She rolled back toward him, opening the condom packet. He took it from her and rolled it on with quick, efficient moves.

He rolled her to her back and positioned himself at the opening of her sex. Claire moaned and writhed as he thrust deep inside her, hard and fast. She wrapped her legs around his waist, urging him deeper. More. He gave it all willingly.

When that wasn't enough, she looped one of those impossibly long legs up and over his shoulder, and then the other. He had to support her hips, and she was unable to move very far, but the penetration was deep. Claire shivered and moaned beneath him. He took her to the brink, and then slowed, willing her climax to slow and grow.

He watched her face as she shattered beneath him, her blue eyes glowing and skin flushed pink with exertion. She shuddered, and he kissed her hard, and buried himself in her as he took his own release.

Their bodies stilled, and they lay together, no longer joined but with their legs and arms intertwined. Helmut's head rested in the crook of Claire's neck. He nuzzled her ear, reveling in her sweet scent. He could feel the rise and fall of her chest as her breathing slowed. They stayed that way for many heartbeats.

Normally, by this point, he was halfway dressed. Making his excuses. Giving empty compliments. Platitudes. Helmut didn't want to move. And no empty words came to mind.

The soft buzzing of a cell phone broke their reverie. Claire broke away and rolled out of bed to answer it. Helmut lay back for a moment, pretending not to listen as she snatched up her phone from the dresser.

She tossed a frown over her shoulder as she answered it, walking out of the bedroom area. Her voice carried over the open walls, but he really wasn't interested in eavesdropping.

This was his cue. With a heavy sigh, he got out of the bed, collected his clothes, and went into the adjacent bathroom to clean up.

Chapter 11

"We can't let our personal feelings get in the way of business."

James Sheffield addressed the built-in camera on his laptop with the same pomp and circumstance that he gave to a conference hall. In a starched white shirt, a single button opened at the neck, and a dark colored sport coat, he was dressed for dinner at the country club. But it was only a yard of silk and a slipknot away from his typical boardroom attire.

From the far side of her father's home office desk, Claire had her laptop open with the series of boxes littering her screen, each containing the image of one of the board of directors or the top executives of S&F.

"But this is Helmut Forrester we're talking about. He's the perfect S&F mascot. I bet the guy sleeps with the quarterly reports," Nan Thompson, the only female member of the board, said. The woman looked old enough to be Claire's great-great grandmother, which was made the joke almost funnier. It made Claire's stomach churn.

Given the sudden fake coughing fits on three other little video feeds, Helmut's reputation among women was well known throughout the company.

Claire felt a blush reddening her temples, thankful for the moment that her camera was off. It was only this morning that she and Helmut had had sex in her kitchen. He had more than lived up to his reputation as a great lover. And now that reputation was about to bring down his career.

She hoped like hell that her own reputation wouldn't come crashing down as well.

Sending video from both computers at once, plus all the incoming feeds, was a bit more than her father's Internet connection could handle, so she and her father had agreed to share the one video connection. Claire wanted no miscommunication or dropped connections. This was too important.

She tapped her father on the shoulder and addressed the crowd, hoping that her rosy cheeks could be attributed to a bad color balance on the camera. "The penalties for this kind of infraction include losing our ability to bid on further government contracts, and even jail time. We've been told, informally, that because our company is so new to this arena, that if we act quickly, we will probably get away with a minor fine."

"All that for one little love affair?" asked Nan. "He has a spotless employment record." Several of the other faces nodded.

Thankfully, both her father and the head of HR could both vouch for that. Never once in his years at the company had anyone ever lodged a complaint. Thankfully, Helmut had appeared to choose his dates from other departments, never sleeping with anyone in his own chain of command.

Until this morning. The thought burned both hot and cold at the same time as she realized just how stupid of a decision she had made. Sleeping with her own employee.

"Everyone please listen to me. What James and I are proposing is *because* of his spotless employment record. If this accusation were made against just about anyone else, we wouldn't be nearly so generous."

James nudged Claire out of the way. "Ladies and gentlemen, you all know that Helmut and I are friends. We play golf together. We have dinner together."

Claire cringed, imagining her father and Helmut sharing stories over a couple of drinks, talking about women. Did Helmut brag about his latest conquests? Had he bragged about this one?

James continued. "This isn't some kind of witch hunt. But the government accountability office has near irrefutable proof that he got way too friendly with an estimator on the other side. They aren't accusing him of outright bribing the gal to help us win the bid for Shadow Fly. Yet."

"So what," another of the board members interrupted. "We're not allowed to be friendly with our customers? That's just business."

"What he did went way beyond business," Claire said from behind her father. "He was romantically involved with this woman during the bidding process. There are laws on the books to prevent companies from corrupting government officials for a reason."

James did not budge from his spot in front of the camera, so Claire gave up and switched on her own. For a moment, all of the faces on her screen froze in place, a grotesque and comical array of half-formed expressions.

"The severance package we are proposing is beyond generous," she said once she got the communications established. "And if we're lucky, that's all we'll lose out of this. HR and Legal are still working on the final wording of the deal. I'll email to you all the moment I receive it."

"Folks," said James over the top of Claire. "Sign it and send it back. Tonight. We need this wrapped up first thing in the morning, before the press gets hold of it. As always, if there's a leak, I'll know where it's coming from."

Claire fumed as she and her father switched off their video connections. Every time she opened her mouth to speak, he had stepped in front of her and taken over.

He stood and yawned. "See, CJ. That's how these things are handled. Now let's get some dinner."

"Is that it? Send some emails, fire your CFO, and then have a steak?" Her voice sounded shrill to her own ears.

He narrowed his eyes. "It's business. Helmut will understand. And we're keeping your stepmother waiting."

She stood up and crossed her hands over her chest and glared. "Let her wait. After all, it's business, right? Business first and foremost. Always."

"What's gotten into you tonight?" He planted his fists on his hips and glared right back.

I know this scene. This is where my father and I have a big loud argument and stop talking for a year. But this time, Claire wouldn't stomp off to her room and rage. Why the hell had she ever thought she could work with her father?

"You're handling way too much," she said through gritted teeth. "This was my problem, not yours. I'm the CEO, remember?"

"But you need board approval to remove another executive from office," he fired back.

"Yes, but I didn't need you to talk for me. What am I, sixteen years old?"

James frowned at Claire. She frowned right back. Finally he threw up his hands.

"For crying out loud, no, you're not sixteen. And stop looking at me like that. You remind me of your mother."

"Then maybe you should have chosen someone else to do this job. Or kept it for yourself. Why bother retiring if you're going to continue to run the company through someone else?" Claire kept herself from shouting the words. Barely.

She had thought this could work. She really had. After all, he had called her, asking if she would accept the position. It wasn't like she had come crawling to Daddy to ask for a handout. But she hadn't intended on butting heads. Or letting him steamroll her.

"The board chose a candidate we thought could handle the responsibility. Were we all wrong?" he asked.

"How the hell would you know? You haven't let me say a complete sentence without interrupting me."

James opened his mouth and then closed it again. Claire stared him down. She wasn't sixteen anymore. And she wouldn't be crying off to her room anymore either. It had been years since their last yelling fight, and her father would have to learn that she'd grown. And hardened.

"Fine," he said, tight-lipped. "It's all yours. Have fun firing your CFO tomorrow, and prepping for the air show next week. Diana wanted to leave for France earlier than normal this year, anyway — something about a trunk show. After I get that severance contract signed, I'm officially on vacation. But you better hope you don't need another emergency board while I'm gone."

"I'm sure I can manage," she said to his back as he stalked out of the room.

What on earth did I just do? Claire stuffed her laptop back into her briefcase and rushed out the door. Her father and his wife had planned all week to take her out to dinner and celebrate her new job. But she couldn't stomach it. As she rode down the elevators from the penthouse condo, she breathed a ragged sigh.

Getting her father to back down was a small victory. But the price might be more than she could stomach.

She now had to find the words to fire the man she'd spent the morning making love to.

"Have you ever been to Jamaica, Claire?" Helmut asked as soon as the office door closed behind him.

The glitter in his eyes sent a thrill of primal lust straight to her core, and she felt her panties growing damp at the memory of his hands on her body. His lips. His tongue.

She looked away.

Even from across the huge monstrosity of a desk Father had left in the office, her nose detected a hint of Helmut's cologne. If she weren't already sitting, the spicy sent would have turned her knees to jelly. She shifted her weight, uncrossing her knees and then crossing her ankles. Failing to find the cool poise that she needed. *What happens on the weekend doesn't have to come to the office on Monday.* Yeah, right.

"Funny that you mention Jamaica." She motioned toward the chair on the other side of her desk.

He relaxed backwards in the tufted leather guest chair and crossed his right ankle over his left knee. "Is that a 'no'? The weather is downright celestial this time of year. There's a tiny, exclusive guesthouse near Negril. Their chef is the best on the island, and the infinity pool commands a view of the entire cove. I would love to take you there."

Claire pictured Helmut swimming in a sparkling blue ocean, the sun glinting off his tanned chest as he ripped through the water. *Get a grip. Focus.* She flipped open the manila folder in front of her and glanced over the top page. One word stood out. *Jamaica.*

"Is this the same beach house that you took Juliana Morgan to last April?" she asked, keeping her voice low. She had to keep a clear head here.

Helmut stiffened visibly, and then smiled. It was a half-smile, more of a quirk of the lips. "Don't worry about Juliana. We went our separate ways months ago."

So it was true. Claire's heart sank. She had such a small thread of hope when she walked in this morning. Maybe it was all a huge misunderstanding. "You invited her on a vacation?"

Helmut dropped his ankle from his knee, and sat up straighter, clearly not amused by her questions. But he kept his smile easygoing. "Yes, I did. I have a contact with a villa in the south of Spain. Would that be more to your taste?"

Spain? What was he thinking? "Helmut, did you pay for Juliana's trip? Plane tickets, meals?"

"Of course," he said, frowning. "I was raised a gentleman. But I am a modern gentleman. We could share expenses, if that would make things more comfortable."

Claire looked agape at Helmut. Did he really believe this conversation was about the possibility of a romantic vacation?

The buzz of his cell phone reverberated in the office, sounding more obnoxious than any blaring hip-hop song. He quickly silenced the thing without even looking.

"Venice?" he offered hopefully. "Have you ever sipped champagne in a gondola?"

Claire put down her pen and took a drink of her quickly cooling coffee. It was too sweet, but it gave her an excuse to delay. And to compose her next words.

"We are the primary contractor on the Shadow Fly project, correct?" she asked.

"Yes. If you want details, you'll have to call in Ben. I'm just the numbers guy, remember?" He looked annoyed, but she had to finish this.

"And that Juliana Morgan worked on the team that awarded us that contract?"

Helmet clenched his jaw. "Of course I knew. How do you think we met?"

She dropped her gaze to her notes. "The contract was awarded May 15. Three weeks after you returned from your jaunt to Jamaica."

"Your point?" He raised one eyebrow in challenge.

"Have you ever heard of the law governing kickbacks?"

"Kickbacks...what are you implying?" Helmut's voice lowered dangerously. "Do you think I bribed Juliana with a trip to Jamaica?"

Claire recoiled at the intense fury she saw in his eyes, but she didn't back down. This was her job, whether she liked it or not. "It certainly looks that way. At least to the government oversight committee."

Helmut sputtered. "We didn't even discuss business on that trip. It was just a vacation. Two consenting adults who enjoyed each other's company. No contracts involved. When the hell did this come about?"

"The other bidder filed a complaint with the government oversight committee just before the close of business on Friday. One of the committee members told us yesterday, as a courtesy. An inquiry isn't slated to start until later this—"

"Yesterday?" His eyes flashed.

Claire lowered her gaze again. She'd gotten the call while she was still in bed with Helmut. And then he practically snuck out of her condo while she was still on the phone. She should have stopped him. Could have stopped him. Could have told him all this up front. But she hadn't wanted her father to know that Helmut was at her house. Besides, she thought the whole thing was some grotesque joke at first.

"I have already talked to the committee chairman, and they agree with me that it was probably an innocent coincidence," she said carefully.

"Damn straight."

Claire gulped. This was it. "However, if we do nothing, they won't let us off the hook. The usual consequence for a company's first time offense is to suspend our right to bid on contracts for six months. In exchange, we have to educate our employees about business ethics, and what behaviors constitute an appearance of impropriety—"

Helmut snorted. "What is this, the eighteenth century? Appearance of impropriety?"

Claire held up one hand, cutting him off. "There's another condition. Your termination."

Helmut sprang to his feet. "My what? You can't fire me. I know this company better than anyone besides James."

"I am aware of that, Helmut," she said quietly. Horribly, embarrassingly aware of it. She might have an intuition for diplomacy, and a knack for leadership and for fostering productivity among her employees. But she had been painfully aware for the past week that it would be years—decades—before she could match Helmut's breadth of knowledge of all aspects of this business.

"I'm the CFO. Only the board can—"

"They have already voted. They are offering you a generous severance package if you will voluntarily resign. It's all spelled out in here—"

Helmut ignored her outstretched hand. She set the folder down on the desk in front of him.

"I will not go quietly," he spat. "And James will hear about this. What do you think he will say about you firing me after we—"

"Don't finish that, Helmut," she warned. "Father knows. About Juliana and the Shadow Fly contract, I mean. He's the chairman of the board. He drafted the severance package himself. Please don't make this personal. This has nothing to do with you and me—"

Helmut spun on his heel and stalked out of the office.

Claire jumped to her feet and tried to follow him. He pushed past Steph, nearly knocking her down. Helmut's jacket sleeve brushed a stack of papers off of a filing cabinet, scattering them on the floor at Claire's feet. He didn't look back.

"That went well," Steph said.

Claire gave a wistful glance as his retreating back. "Yeah. Right."

"I take it something happened. Between you two?"

Claire knelt down and began stacking papers. Neatly. Perfectly. Ensuring that each one was aligned just so with the one below it. She took a deep, shuddering breath.

Steph bent down next to Claire and scooped all of them, including Claire's stack, into a loose heap. "That bad, huh."

"It's complicated."

Claire had a feeling it was going to take a long time before she, and Sheffield and Fox, finished picking up the pieces of this mess.

This was the first time he'd ever been fired.

"Asked to resign." Ben took a hearty swig of his beer.

"Same damn thing," Helmut sputtered defensively. He gulped the shot of whiskey—his fourth in under an hour — and clanked the heavy crystal down on the mahogany bar. The bartender didn't even glance up from the stack of glasses he was polishing at the far end. A hefty up-front tip should have assured Helmut good service, and the bar on the ground floor of the Ritz Carlton was all but deserted at ten a.m. on a Monday.

Helmut raised one arm and snapped his fingers. The bartender glanced his direction, and strode purposefully down the length of the room. Helmut shoved his glass toward the man.

"Might I offer you a soda, sir?"

"No, goddammit. I want another whiskey. Do I look like I want a goddamned soda?"

"No sir," the bartender replied smoothly as he filled a glass with ice and then Coke from the nozzle. He set the full glass next to Helmut's empty double old-fashioned. "But this one is on the house."

"What do I look like, some kind of fucking drunk?"

"Of course not, sir. Are you a guest of the hotel, sir? Could I perhaps call a bellhop to assist you to your room?"

"Helmut," Ben interrupted. Ben looked irritatingly amused by the whole scene. "Give the guy a break. They probably have some corporate policy —"

"Fuck corporate policy. Fuck him and fuck you, Ben. You're probably getting a promotion out of all this bullshit. And what the hell do I have? Nothing."

Ben set his beer down quietly on the bar. His voice remained calm, and his expression mild. "I wouldn't call nine months full pay plus stock options 'nothing.' Think of it this way, you can spend the next year sitting on a beach, sipping rum and screwing the señoritas while I'm working 90-hour weeks."

Helmut took a gulp of the soda. He didn't want to talk about beaches and señoritas.

"Or, better yet, invest some of that money into that business plan you've been mooning over for the last five years. This is probably the best damned thing to happen to you, Helmut."

It was the best thing to happen to Ben. With Helmut gone, Ben's boss was the logical choice for the CFO spot, which put Ben in charge of the entire rotorcraft division.

"Too bad you didn't screw the bitch yet," Ben continued between gulps.

It took Helmut a minute to understand Ben's meaning. "Why do you say that?"

"Lawsuit city, Helmut. What did she call it? The 'appearance of impropriety?' How 'proper' would it be if she got caught fucking her executive team?" Ben laughed at his own cleverness. "By the way, man, you owe me a thousand bucks."

Helmut lifted his glass and gave it a swirl, entranced by how the carbonation bubbles danced in the fine crystal. He'd nearly forgotten about the stupid bet. Pursuing Claire had become the goal itself, instead of the means to an end. He tried to recall just when he'd lost his focus, but all he could remember was a pair of clear blue eyes glowing in pleasure.

"It's been great, buddy," Ben said as he pushed back his barstool and set the empty beer bottle on the counter. "But I've got a job to get back to."

If he weren't so damned drunk, Helmut would have replied with some witty remark. Probably comparing the size of Ben's dick with that of a small rodent. "Hey, Ben," he said.

"Yeah, Helmut?"

"My two weeks aren't over yet."

Chapter 12

Helmut was everywhere but by her side. Claire sipped her Bordeaux and made small talk with yet another French private airline executive.

"Non, non, Mademoiselle Sheffield," a short, bald man said. "We do not buy refurbished planes, no matter how luxurious."

The half dozen middle-aged men standing around her burst into a heated multi-lingual debate over the emerging market for refurbished jets in Eastern Europe. Even if she could understand the swirling French and Italian discussion, her mind was anywhere but on business.

Steph had warned her that she had no time in her schedule for jetlag, and the marathon of executive breakfasts, press conferences, VIP lunches, and cocktail parties weighed on her.

The Paris Air Show was one of the industry's most prestigious—and most exhausting—events. Held only every other year, all of the major players in aerospace had a presence at the week-long conference. There were daily air shows, a convention hall the size of three football fields, and endless opportunities for networking.

Tonight, it was not the dizzying number of new faces and business cards that she had exchanged that weighed on her. It was the constant, haunting presence of a pair of gray-green eyes that followed her every move.

Why is he here?

His sudden departure from Sheffield & Fox was a minor scandal in the business world. Her feet had barely touched French soil on Tuesday before reporters from the Wall Street Journal, Business Weekly, and Fox News had thrust microphones under her nose, demanding that she elaborate on the tersely worded notice of his departure.

Claire heard Helmut's deep laughter echo across the small reception room. She stiffened her shoulders. Everywhere she went, it seemed, he was there, too. Chatting with her suppliers and competitors like they were old pals. Heads together with various government heads — higher-ups from the FAA, and the British and French equivalents. He knew everyone.

That was the biggest rub. Even Claire's memory for names and faces was taxed by meeting hundreds of Important Contacts in two days. With virtually no sleep. And Helmut seemed to know them all. He would have been the perfect person to have by her side, to help with introductions and smooth over awkward silences. But he talked to everyone in the room except her.

This was some kind of damned vacation for the man.

Claire's calves ached from the spike-heeled Monolo Blahniks she wore with her black Anne Klein cocktail dress. Suddenly her vision went blurry, and she frowned at the balloon wine glass in her hand.

Networking opportunity or no, she had to sleep.

She politely excused herself from the debate and headed toward the door. They barely seemed to notice her departure.

Before she could reach the hallway that led back toward the main portion of the hotel, Claire's small black clutch vibrated. She pulled her cell phone out of the evening bag and frowned at the urgent flag on an incoming email. She clicked the button to read it as she walked.

A crisp white shirt and the olive tweed of a sport coat slammed into Claire's vision. She squealed in surprise as she ran straight into a man's broadly muscled chest. Her phone and evening bag skittered to the floor and she clutched at the lapels of his jacket as one of her narrow-heeled shoes twisted out from under her.

"Whoa," a deep baritone said as strong hands gripped her around the waist, steadying her.

"I'm so sorry. I wasn't looking where I was going," she sputtered, and then stopped. She recognized the warm spicy scent of Helmut's cologne before she lifted her gaze to his laughing eyes.

"Fancy running into you here," he said, still holding her close to his body.

The heat of his hands burned her through the smooth silk of her dress, and she fought the urge to melt into those familiar arms.

"Let go, Helmut." Claire put the palms of her hands on his chest and pushed lightly. He relinquished a scant inch.

"How is your first Air Show?" His eyes swept downward, lingering on the swell of her breasts.

Claire's nipples hardened, the peaks straining against the layers of bra and gown. Desire pooled in her lower abdomen, making her knees weak. It annoyed the hell out of her. "It's nice to see you, too, Helmut," she said through gritted teeth. "Don't create a scene. Please."

"No, we can't have that. It would be such a shame to drag the lofty name of Sheffield & Fox through the mud."

Claire peeled his fingers from her waistline. She backed away from the acrid tone of his voice as much as the longing she felt to wrap herself around this man. She had already risked the reputation she was building for herself in the industry once. Giving in again now would be worse than foolish.

"Mademoiselle."

A black and white clad waiter materialized next to Claire, calmly holding her purse and cell phone. Claire took a deep, refreshing breath and smoothed the fabric of her skirt. She took her things and thanked the waiter with a hasty "Merci."

"Good night, Helmut." She lifted her head high and staunchly refused to glance at the cocktail reception behind her. If anyone had noticed her scene, she would not add jet fuel to the fire by looking guilty.

"Do you mind if I walk with you?" Helmut fell into step beside her without waiting for a reply. "How are you enjoying the Air Show?"

"Didn't we already cover that?" Claire rounded the corner into the hotel's main lobby, her heels clanking obnoxiously on the marble tiled floor. She longed to slip them off and ease the cramps forming in her arches.

"You never answered."

She punched the up button on the elevator and rubbed her bare arms against the chill of the room.

"Why are *you* here, Helmut?"

"I found myself with some unexpected free time, and a ticket to Paris. Thought I'd come hang out with some old friends. Maybe look for a job." The elevator doors slid open, and Helmut smiled and stood back, waiting for Claire to enter first.

She glanced nervously around the lobby before the doors closed on the two of them. Alone. No one seemed to be paying them any attention.

"Didn't you turn that ticket in with the rest of the company property?" Claire hated the petulant tone she heard in her own voice.

"Is the company in such bad shape that a couple thousand dollars would bring you down? Sounds like I chose a good time to retire."

With a groan, the elevator began to move. The space felt entirely enclosed, even with the brass-plated walls and ceiling polished to a mirrored shine. Everywhere she looked, she saw Helmut's mocking grin.

"I should have taken the stairs. I think this is the slowest elevator I've ever set foot in," Claire muttered.

"Not everyone likes to fly to the top. Some of us prefer a steady climb," he replied mildly.

She clamped her mouth shut before the wine and exhaustion could make her say something she regretted. She leaned sideways for a moment, resting her hip against the wall and closing her eyes as she waited for the slow ascent to finally finish.

"It can be overwhelming, I know," Helmut said quietly.

Claire peered up at him from under half-closed lashes. He was leaning against the opposite wall, looking relaxed. And pensive. Suspiciously she asked, "What is overwhelming?"

"The Show. The mad crush of people and information. The first time I came, eight years ago as a middle-manager, I felt like a kid at Disney World. Wide-eyed with wonder at all of the possibilities. The technology. The cooperation between companies and countries. The scale of the deals brokered and careers ruined."

The tiny bell of the elevator dinged and the doors slid open with a whoosh. Helmut motioned again for Claire to precede him.

"How did you know what floor my room was on?" She realized she hadn't pressed a button.

"We stay in the same hotel every time. Most of the suites are on this floor. Your father always stayed up here. I guessed you would, too."

Claire nodded. Her room reservation had originally been made in his name. Her father and stepmother had rented a townhouse not far away instead. She wanted to think he had given away the reservation so that she could have easy access to some of her meetings. More likely, it was about the parties her stepmother wanted to host.

"Good night, Claire." Helmut's expression had lost its smirk.

For half a heartbeat, she considered asking him back to her room, foolish and desperate as the invitation would look. But he was already heading down the opposite corridor without so much as a backward glance.

Claire sighed as she hobbled down to the last door and slid her key card into the lock.

She kicked off her shoes, dropped her clutch onto a table, and collapsed onto a slate-gray suede sofa in the suite's sitting room.

It wasn't until her evening bag vibrated, announcing another message, that she remembered the email she had started to read when she ran into Helmut downstairs.

Chapter 13

Helmut paced the length of his room. His gut tightened into a knot, and his fingers clenched into fists. His heart thudded impatiently in his chest, blood simmering. When he'd held Claire's body in his hands down in the reception hall, it was all he could do not to sweep her into a dark corner and free those beautiful curves from the confining little dress.

Get a grip. He had boarded the red-eye out of O'Hare Monday night still ripe with righteous anger and buzzing from the two shots of bourbon he'd downed in the airport bar before takeoff.

The plan was simple. He would breeze into Paris and whisk the vixen with her long legs and wickedly beautiful eyes back to his hotel room, where he could douse the fire of his desire by burying himself between those legs.

Winning the bet with Ben would not be his primary objective. Hell, he'd already won, though Ben would want proof before he parted with one red cent. But the money wasn't the problem either. Ben was right. Helmut could easily afford to take a year—or five—off. His finances were secure.

The biggest irony of this whole affair was that he spent money on women because he had so little else in his life to spend it on. And even lavishing his dates with expensive dinners and weekend getaways didn't amount to much of a dent in his wallet.

With most of the women he'd dated over the past ten years, the passion was short-lived. Quickly snuffed once he realized that he had nothing in common with them when their clothes were on. Even damned Juliana, his longest relationship in years, had only lasted a month before they parted.

And then Claire arrived on the scene. Beautiful. Sexy. Passionate. Intelligent. And a keen instinct for business.

When he stepped off the plane in Paris, he was greeted by Claire's face on the national news, calmly smoothing over Helmut's sudden departure from the company. Downplaying the inquiries into their Shadow Fly negotiations. His mistakes. Mistakes that could lose the company both the contract and the chance to bid on future work. Never once blaming, or insinuating, any guilt on Helmut's part.

He could kick himself for being so stupid. When he pursued Juliana, he was thinking only of spending a little time with a beautiful woman. He should have known that the affair could jeopardize the negotiations.

Hell, he did know. He just didn't give a damn at the time.

Helmut had been married to his job at Sheffield and Fox for as long as he could remember. Reporting for work, for him, was like coming home. It was comfortable. Safe. And lonely. Maybe he'd been tempting fate when he dated Juliana. Daring someone to call him on his juvenile behavior, and his blatant disregard for ethics.

He hadn't expected that whistle-blower to be Claire. He hadn't expected there to *be* a Claire in his life. In a little under two weeks, the woman had turned his life upside down and backwards.

He had ducked the reporters as best he could, and gave only the most banal answers when he couldn't. His schedule for the week had been full when he was still an S&F employee. Arriving as a free agent had tripled the number of invitations, despite the looming investigation. He knew he had lots of friends in the industry. And it amused the hell out of him to be blatantly courted by his competitors. No, Sheffield & Fox's competitors. Most of them were probably hoping that if they hired him, he'd bring a little insider knowledge with him. He couldn't blame them for the assumption. He hadn't exactly proven himself virtuous of late.

Helmut stalked to the mini bar and yanked the fridge door open. Wine, vodka, soda. Nothing appealed. He slammed the door shut again.

He should get out. Go for a run on a treadmill in the fitness center. Call a few of the guys for a night on the town. Knock on Claire's door and beg her for mercy. She was everywhere, with her sexy laugh and her cool poise. She attracted flocks of men at every meet-and-greet. Executives, government officials, ridiculously rich playboys posing as potential investors. All vied for the chance to stand in her spotlight.

She was a contrast in silk and steel, youth and wisdom. She was irresistible.

The pounding in Helmut's head was not a headache. It was his door.

It was Claire. Still wearing the slinky black dress, and barefoot. And wielding a cell phone like a butcher's knife aimed at his heart.

"Where the hell do you get off threatening me this way?" she demanded, storming into his room, leaving a trail of coconuts and sweetness in her wake.

"I have no idea what you're talking about."

She whirled and planted fists on her hips. Helmut's gaze traveled the length of her. She had removed not only her shoes, but her stockings as well. He suppressed a groan at the sight of her bare legs.

"The email you sent. You've got about thirty seconds to explain yourself before I call the FBI."

He wrenched his eyes back to her accusing glare. "Claire, I didn't send any email. What are you talking about?"

"'If you don't cancel the demo of Shadow Fly, someone will get hurt,'" she read, her voice dripping acid. "Signed H.A.F. And sent from an anonymous Yahoo account."

"Claire, calm down. I didn't send any email. And I'm not 'H.A.F.' My middle initial's D, not A." He frowned. "It's probably some kind of prank. Or spam."

"This cell phone is new." Claire's voice wavered. Just a little. "I had to change the number when I added international service. The only people I sent the address to were the executive team."

Helmut quietly closed the door to the suite. There was no need to share this discussion with the entire hotel floor. "Call the FBI. Or at least the IT department. It looks like you've been hacked."

"Why now? Why target Shadow Fly?"

Helmut shrugged. "I don't know. Anything government related is always a target. And Sheffield & Fox has been in the news this week."

Claire wrapped her arms around her chest and took a visible breath. Good. She looked like she was calming down.

"Call your IT folks. Where's your assistant? She seemed pretty sharp. She could follow up on this for you."

Claire shook her head. "Steph is in Chicago. Couldn't get her passport updated on such short notice."

Helmut glanced at his watch. Six p.m. "Call her. It's noon in Chicago. Sit, Claire, and call. You won't relax until you do." He motioned toward the navy blue sofa. To his relief, she sat.

He busied himself at the wet bar, pouring two glasses of plain bottled water. He might have preferred the wine, but between the cocktail hour and jetlag, Claire already looked on the verge of collapse. He waited until he heard her say goodbye and click off her phone.

She had tucked her feet up underneath her, and it reminded Helmut of the first night they met, when he brought her Chinese food to her father's office. Her office. She looked just as young now, and ten times as vulnerable. But now he also recognized the titanium that ran through her spine.

"What is this?" she asked, accepting the glass.

"Plain water." He eyed the expanse of upholstery next to her, and pictured her lounging across it. Naked. He turned back to the bar to retrieve his own glass. Putting several feet between them didn't help.

She raised one eyebrow. "You're pulling out all the stops."

"You're too trusting."

"Oh?" She raised the water to her lips and took a small sip.

"You thought I was threatening to harm somebody, so you came rushing to my room. Alone. Unarmed. And barefoot." The thought sent chills down his spine.

She flushed a deep pink, the color creeping downward across her chest.

"I guess I..." she stammered, shifting her feet so that one calf dangled down over the edge of the chair. "I didn't really think you wanted to hurt anyone. I thought it was some kind of..."

Helmut set his jaw, and walked past her to the suite door. "Some kind of what, Claire?" He opened the door, and motioned toward it.

She stood, setting her water down on the small ebony-colored sofa table behind her. "I thought it was some trick to get my attention," she said quietly, stopping in front of him. "I'm sorry."

Helmut gulped. She stood just inches from him. He could hear her quickened breath. Without those sexy heels she had on earlier, he could look down and see the top of her head, soft blond hair in slight disarray.

"If I'd wanted to get your attention," he said thickly, "I wouldn't have sent an anonymous email."

She looked up and their eyes met. "What would you have done?" she asked.

"This."

He snaked one hand around her waist and pulled her hard against him for a kiss. The other hand slammed the door shut and then wrapped around her bottom, sliding down until he found the hem of her dress and gently tugging upwards.

Claire moaned against his mouth, their tongue meshing as she stood on her toes and pressed herself against him. Helmut reached his other hand down and ran both of them up those delectably bare legs until they found equally bare hips. His thumbs found the skimpy fabric of a thong and with a swift tug slipped it down and to the floor.

"My dress," she moaned against his mouth.

"Mmmm... It's lovely," he said as his fingers found her hot center.

She mewled as he stroked the damp opening and she gasped as he slipped one finger inside her. She clasped both arms around his neck and arched her head backwards in pleasure as he stroked her.

Helmut's cock strained against his pants as she ground her hips upwards, urging his hand deeper. He trailed kisses down her neck, and she lifted one thigh up and wrapped it around his back.

"The dress, Helmut," she gasped as he nibbled the sensitive spot behind her ear.

"Would look better on the floor," he said.

He withdrew his hand and silenced her protest with another searing kiss. Then he supported her bottom with his arms and lifted her other thigh up to wrap around his waist. He tucked her chin onto his shoulder as he carried her into the adjoining bedroom.

He let go of her. She slid her legs down to the floor, and then turned her back to him.

Claire lifted her hair from the nape of her neck, and Helmut kissed it. He wrapped his hands around under her arms to cup her breasts and gently squeeze.

"Zipper," she said, panting.

Helmut grinned and kissed the bone at the base of her neck. He found her nipples through the layers of fabric and gently pinched them between his thumb and forefinger. "Ask nicely," he asked, loving the feel of her naked bottom against his groin.

"Please."

He obliged, slowly lowering the zipper down the center of her back, licking every newly exposed inch of skin along the way. He had to kneel as he exposed the small of her back. Finally he pulled the short sleeves down over her arms, and lowered the dress and allowed her to step out of it. He unhooked her bra with a quick flick of his fingers, and tossed the garment aside.

Claire tried to turn around, but he held her hips still. "I like this view," he whispered, and nudged her knees apart.

He could feel the shiver that ran down her spine as he trailed his fingers up the insides of her thighs. "Lean forward for me."

She bent forward and rested her hands on the side of the bed in front of her. "Like this?"

"Perfect." From his knees, he could easily see her lips, swollen and wet, spread before him. He found her clit with his fingers and stroked, until she was panting again and thrusting her hips against him. He kissed the smooth skin of her buttocks as he slid one finger and then two inside of her.

Claire whimpered and moaned, her fingers twisting in the sheets, her hips undulating against his hands. He held her still as he felt the contractions ripple over her.

Carefully, he let go of her.

"Helmut?" she whispered with a groan.

"Stay there." He quickly removed his shirt and pants. His cock was hard and throbbing. The sight of her naked backside bent over the bed, wet and ready, was almost too much. He found a condom from his pants pocket and rolled it down his hard length.

He positioned himself at her entrance and gripped her hips, the tip of his cock nudging her lips apart. Claire moaned and lifted her hips, urging him inward.

With a groan, he thrust inside her, and she whimpered. He paused, afraid that he had gone too fast. "Don't stop," she gasped, wriggling her hips.

Helmut needed no further encouragement. He thrust into her again and again, and she met each movement with her own.

"More," she gasped, her hand sliding down to work her own clit.

Helmut leaned forward, pulling her up against the length of his bare torso. One hand played with her nipples, squeezing and tugging. The other displaced her hand to stroke her clit from the front while he slid in and out of her tight, wet sheath.

He felt her climax building. Her head thrashed side to side and she whimpered and moaned. Her entire body was liquid fire in his arms. Helmut buried his face in her hair and clung to her as she came apart in his arms. He then shuddered as he came inside her.

Helmut cradled her against his chest as their breathing slowed. After a moment, he gently slid out of her and lifted her in his arms.

"Where are we going?" she asked.

"The same place we've been trying to get to. The bed."

She giggled as he gently tossed her onto the now rumpled covers and climbed in beside her. The sound tickled over him and he grinned down at her, feeling freer than he had in a long time.

The sight of her bare breasts distracted him from examining that thought any more deeply. He kissed each one of them thoroughly, gently sucking on the nipples as his fingers played over the delicate bones of her rib cage.

She sighed.

He gasped as her fingers closed around his already hardening shaft.

"What, not ready for more yet?" she asked with a breathy feigned innocence.

"Getting there," he said and closed his eyes as she cupped his balls. "You're killing me."

"Hmm..." she said, and squeezed his cock. "Your blood pressure seems fine."

Helmut captured her lips for a long, hard kiss as he leisurely explored the curves of her waistline and abdomen.

"I do have one question," she said when their lips parted again. Her hands trailed up over his chest. His cock was fully erect again, pressing against the curls between her legs.

"What's that?" he said, and lowered his head to place a kiss on her sternum.

"What does the D stand for?"

Helmut raised his gaze and looked into her eyes. They sparkled with desire and curiosity.

"David."

She laughed.

"What's so funny about the name 'David'?" he asked.

"I don't know." She giggled. "I guess I was expecting something a bit more...unusual. To go along with Helmut."

He grinned. "I was named after my grandfathers. My mom's father was a German draft dodger during World War II. That's where I got Helmut. My dad's father was an Iowa farmer. David. Besides, you're a fine one to talk."

"Me?" she asked and then gasped as he cupped her sex with his palm. "Why me?"

"Claire *James*."

"Mmmm..." was all she said as he slid his fingers inside her again.

The purple haze of dawn was just filtering through the heavy hotel drapes when he felt her stir. Helmut squinted at the alarm clock next to the bed. Five a.m.

The hourglass curve of her bare back tempted his fingers. With one soft caress, perhaps he could coax her warm length up against his hips. Her butt snuggled up against the erection that was beginning to swell.

Noiselessly she sat up, careful not to ruffle the sheets, and slipped her legs over the side of the bed. Helmut narrowed his eyes and watched her through his lashes, not moving. Willing his breath to stay even and slow.

Claire quietly gathered up her discarded clothes and padded out the bedroom door to the sitting area beyond. He heard the soft rustling and telltale zip of her cocktail dress, and then the soft click of the door to the hallway as she crept out without a word, or a backwards glance.

Just like I did. Whoever coined the phrase "turnabout is fair play" should be guillotined.

Helmut buried his head in the pillow, still smelling of her tropical shampoo. The bed sheets beside him were cooling rapidly without Claire's heat, and his cock pulsed angrily between his legs as the word "turnabout" conjured images of her bent over the foot of the bed last night.

Chapter 14

The townhouse her father had rented had a carved stone façade, black wrought iron balconies on every window, and a carved mahogany door that slid open silently, despite its apparent weight.

"Claire, dear, welcome. You look tired." Claire's stepmother, Diana, eyed Claire's slightly rumpled linen skirt suit.

Claire suppressed the urge to roll her eyes, and fixed a polite smile on her face. As greetings went, that was one of the nicer things Diana had ever said to her. "The house is lovely."

Diana shrugged cashmere-draped shoulders and gently tossed her head, causing two sparkly earrings to bob beneath her perfectly up-swept chocolate brown hair. "It's passable. I had hoped for the little chalet that we rented a few years back, but the new owners were not entertaining offers. Marie! Come take mademoiselle's coat."

Claire handed her trench over to a black-and-white clad maid, and suppressed a second eye roll. If there were an actual castle for rent in the city of Paris, Diana would have snapped it up, and insisted on a coach-and-four instead of a town car.

"When did you go brunette, Diana?" she asked instead, noting how Diana's eyebrows had been dyed the exact same shade as her hair, and that expertly applied concealer could not totally cover fine lines appearing at the corner of the woman's eyes. Her father's wife was only twelve years older than Claire, and until recently had always been a perfectly tanned, perfectly bleached, blonde.

"I did it last week in honor of your father's retirement." Diana patted the sides of her up-do with a tiny flourish of her fingers that set her rings sparkling in the morning light. "He is in the salon talking with a certain *someone*, if you catch my drift. Go on in, and tell James that I will join you all soon."

Did Diana just wink? Claire frowned as she walked toward the archway at the end of the two-story vestibule. She paused on the threshold, heart caught in her throat.

Champagne flute in one hand, Helmut leaned comfortably against the stone mantle at the far end of the room. She hadn't known he was invited to her father's brunch this morning. And she had slipped back to her hotel room while he was still asleep.

Foolish of her not to ask.

Helmut had worked for Father for years. Hell, her father probably golfed with the man she'd spent hours shagging last night. The mental picture of Helmut and Father joking about women over a beer and a mulligan made her very uncomfortable.

Helmut glanced up and their eyes met across the wide expanse of chintz-covered furniture and Persian rugs. The white-hot heat in that gaze flew straight to Claire's core, and warmth spread down toward her knees. She took a steadying breath and stepped lightly into the room.

"Claire, dear, look who's here."

Claire pulled up short at the gravelly bass of her father's voice. James lounged in an incongruously delicate blue slipper chair, opposite Frank. Her slime of an ex-fiancé grinned up at her from a matching chair. "What are you doing here, Frank?"

"Surprise," Frank said as he got to his feet. "When Diana found out that I was in town, she insisted that I come for brunch today. You look beautiful, Claire."

Claire stood stiffly as he stepped forward and kissed her on the cheek. His temples were slightly flushed and his breath smelled of red wine. She could feel his hot palms through the sleeves of her jacket, and she pulled back away from the embrace. "I need to talk to you, Father."

James stood with a sigh. "What, no hello for your dad? Don't tell me you're still sore about the conference call?"

"It's important."

"Frank, if you'll excuse us. I think I know what this is about." He shot Frank a knowing look and placed a hand around Claire's shoulders to lead her to a small side door. "There's a little study over here that I've claimed for myself for the week. We can talk there."

The small room looked like a medieval king's solar, with rough-hewn stone walls, red and cream tapestries, and a massive carved wooden desk chair that looked more like a throne than office furniture. Claire waited until the door clicked shut behind them before she pounced. "How could you have invited him?"

James crossed his arms across his chest. Even with a receding hairline and a slight paunch, he was still a good-looking man. "Now, don't get so upset. We're all adults here and your stepmother and I enjoy his company."

"After what he did? You could have at least warned me." She drew herself up to her full height. In heels, she just looked her father in the eye. And if he felt a little disconcerted by the level playing field, even better. She was no rebellious teenager any more.

He waved one hand. "Water under the bridge. It was just one affair—"

"One affair?" Claire heard the pitch of her voice escalating and made a conscious effort to control her anger. "That affair cost me—"

"What did it cost you, CJ?" James' voice lowered a notch and his eyes flashed. "Some bad press? A few bucks on the stock price? He's made his mistakes and he's paying for it now. Get over yourself, daughter, and let bygones be bygones."

Claire was taken aback by the venom in her father's voice. She made to step around him back for the door. "Fine. You and Diana are welcome to entertain whoever you choose. Just keep Frank on the other side of the room from me. You may have forgiven him for his 'one affair,' but I haven't."

"Wait, what?" One of James' arms reached out and caught Claire by the elbow. "What is this about Frank?"

Claire stared incredulously at her father. "Didn't you hear me? You might have forgiven my ex-fiancé for his affairs," she said, emphasizing the plural. "But I have not. And I don't care to spend time with him."

"This is about Frank?" he asked, not releasing her arm. "He said you two were reconciling..."

"Who did you think we were arguing about? And no, we're not reconciled. Nor will we be." She gave a small tug on her arm.

James let go of her arm, but turned to block her from reaching the doorknob. His features softened. "I thought you were upset about Helmut. I realized that his affair with that government woman cost the company a lot of embarrassment this week. I saw the look that passed between you two when you walked in the room just now and I thought you were upset to see him."

Claire crossed her arms across her chest and took a steadying breath as her anger began to dissipate. Yes, seeing Helmut under her father's roof made her uncomfortable, but she wasn't about to explain exactly why. She changed the subject. "What line did Frank give you, anyway?"

Her father shrugged helplessly. "You'd have to ask Diana. She is the one who actually arranged it. And please don't be mad at her. You have no idea how had she has tried to make peace with you and your brothers over the years. I wish you would give her a chance."

Claire raised one eyebrow questioningly at her father. Did he really expect her to just run headlong into his scheming wife's motherly embrace and start exchanging girl talk?

"I didn't know." His voice was soft, almost a whisper.

Claire allowed herself one huff and turned back toward the door.

"How bad was it, CJ? Do I need to bodily remove him from the salon? I don't pack my rifle, but there are some vicious-looking swords in a cabinet in the upstairs hall..."

She paused with her hand on the doorknob, and her lips twitched. In high school, her father had threatened one of her dates with a rifle. An unloaded, dusty, Civil War era antique rifle. The kid had been so scared that he wet his pants right there, and never spoke to her again. In return, Claire didn't speak to her father for two whole months. It was funny. Now.

"I outgrew the need for a knight in shining armor a long time ago, Dad. I fight my own battles, now."

"So I've noticed."

Helmut laughed politely at a joke he only half-understood from the mouth of a petite steel-haired lady with a heavy Italian accent, and glanced casually toward the study door. In Claire's quiet departure from his room that morning, there hadn't exactly been time to compare schedules, and he knew she'd be surprised to see him here.

He'd been planning to blow off the invitation, until James had called yesterday.

Not one word of apology from the man. Helmut had not expected one. James had matter-of-factly told Helmut that he had a lead from one of his fellow club members about a vacancy in an auto manufacturer outside Venice.

Signora Ricci's husband and James had been friends since college. The husband was enjoying a breezy retirement full of yachting and deep sea fishing, leaving Signora happily free to focus on driving her family's company to new heights of success. Helmut wasn't sure whether to envy or pity the husband.

"How do you like working for a woman?" Signora asked, setting her china espresso cup sharply onto its saucer.

Helmut blinked. "I, uh, don't. Anymore." He took a quick sip of his Bloody Mary hoping to cover his inattention. She was a direct one. Not sixty seconds ago she'd been talking about her trip to Cambridge to settle her youngest son at Harvard.

She fixed him with a piercing stare. "Si, si, Helmut. I mean in general. If you are half the man that James claims, then you would be a valuable addition to my team."

He heard the study door click open and risked a glance as Claire and James emerged. She was slightly flushed at the cheekbones, and her eyes glowed with the same brightness he'd seen in the boardroom during a debate. Her gaze slid right past him with the barest glance.

"Well?" Signora folded her hands primly on one knee.

Helmut smiled his best meet-the-press smile at the lady. "I've never been to Venice," he said slowly.

She grinned. "It will suit you, I think, Helmut. My assistant will send you the details."

James and Diana ensconced in another corner talking in hushed tones. He couldn't tell what the discussion was about, but Helmut caught Diana tossing him a furtive glance. The next fifteen minutes in the salon reminded Helmut of a chess match, with Claire maneuvering herself as far as possible from both Helmut and Frank, no matter how the rest of the guests circulated.

Signora slipped her arm into Helmut's. "Come sit next to me for the meal, Helmut. I'd like your opinion on these US import laws. How do you think an independent company like mine can work with them to bring our cars to customers?"

Helmut tried to cobble together a decent answer. It wasn't the first time this week that an executive had picked his brain on business strategy. But it was impossible to think straight with Claire across the room avoiding his eyes, Frank alternately mooning over her and glaring at him, and James giving him a furtive thumbs up from behind Signora. It was the most surreal combination of torture and job interview Helmut had ever endured.

He escorted Signora into the dining room, where miniature Eiffel Towers held name cards at the long, stately table. After a quick scan, Helmut saw Claire's and Frank's names arranged side by side.

He allowed Signora Ricci to drag him around the long side of the table and he held out the chair she selected for herself, completely ignoring the seating arrangement. He then sat next to her, and watched as the rest of the guests shuffled around place cards. Claire snatched her own name card and quickly sat between two businessmen. Frank sat awkwardly between Diana and James.

"I think we caused a bit of mayhem with Diana's plans," he whispered to Signora.

She waved one hand dismissively. "What would be the use in attending this sort of thing if we couldn't make the right sorts of connections? James understands."

With each subsequent course, Helmut found himself drawn closer into the idea of Italy. Signora's business wasn't unlike S&F. It was privately owned, but that was a plus in his mind. She had been amassing enough capital and was poised to grow, ready to tap into the American and South American luxury car markets. With a shaky economy, it was a risky venture, but if they could gain a foothold now, they would be secure when things turned around.

If Helmut could have written up his dream job description, this was it.

It was in Italy.

At the far end of the table, Claire laughed at someone's joke, and he remembered how she laughed at his stupid motorcycle stories that first night over Chinese. They had shared very little laughter since that moment, just passion, intensity, and heated debate. Their eyes met briefly across the span of floral centerpieces and crystal juice glasses. Claire looked away first.

Italy might be good for him.

Chapter 15

Claire sighed in relief as Frank said his goodbyes to her stepmother and left. Her stomach ached from the tension, though she'd only picked at the delicious food. Too much coffee, and one unwise mimosa churned in her midsection. Maybe she could grab a plain croissant at the hotel before her afternoon meeting.

As the party broke up, Claire gathered her coat and stepped out onto the steps to wait while the butler hailed her a cab.

"Mind if I ride back with you?"

Claire started. Helmut stood just at the doorway, his own tan raincoat hooked by a finger over his shoulder.

"Taxis seem a bit scarce in this part of town," he said.

Claire glanced over his shoulder toward the tall door as he started down the stairs.

"I don't have to if it bothers you."

She shook her head. "No, it's fine. Why would it bother me?" Though his shoulders were several inches away, she could feel his body heat through the thin fabric of her blouse. She clutched her jacket tighter to her chest.

They waited in awkward silence as a cab pulled forward and the butler opened the door for them. Claire slid across the vinyl seat and then Helmut was closed in beside her, his broad shoulders and long legs dwarfing the tiny space. *Just like after the concert.*

She stared out the window as the view changed from stately homes to close-packed townhouses and apartments. She felt like a kid with her first crush. She'd slept with this man, and had no idea what to say to him.

Good morning. How did you like the blow job last night? Thanks for not telling my father that you made me come five times in three hours. "I didn't know you would be here this morning," she said.

"I should have mentioned the invitation last night."

Their eyes met and she snapped her gaze back to the road. "We didn't really have much time to talk."

His lips quirked. "No, we didn't."

She chanced another glance, and her mouth went dry at the invitation in his eyes. She licked her lips nervously.

"Claire." The word was a caress. A very naughty one.

"And about last week—"

His smile broadened into a full-fledged grin. "Your kitchen is lovely."

Claire blushed. "Not about my kitchen. It's about what happened after. Not *right* after. I mean..."

He raised one eyebrow, eyes sparkling like silvered emeralds as she stammered through her sentence.

She took a breath and started over again. "About your job. I am sorry that you lost your job."

She winced as his eyes turned stony and he turned his gaze out the window. "It happens."

"It wasn't personal. I had to act quickly. The whole board did. None of us were happy about it." She wished he would turn back to face her.

"I can imagine."

"The timing was horrible. But we agreed, before, that what happens outside of the office..."

His gaze flicked back to hers, unreadable this time. "I understand, Claire. Business is business. Personal is personal. You made the right decision, in the circumstances."

Claire bit her tongue. Was the right decision really to let Helmut go, but not disclose her own relationship with a coworker? There was a much-ignored company policy about intra-office dating. Legal made a big deal about shielding the company from sexual harassment charges. It wasn't like there was any chance Helmut would be complaining about that, the way he'd pursued her. But the problem still worried her.

The sound of tires screeching wiped away all chances for further conversation.

With a thud and a crunch, Claire and Helmut were thrown forward against the Plexiglas partition separating them from the driver. Claire threw her hands up just in time to prevent her nose from smashing against the hard surface and she slid downwards onto the floor of the car.

She sat for a moment, stunned. Outside the car, horns honked and car doors slammed.

She took inventory. Her right wrist felt sore from where her hand had caught her, and the top of her forehead felt bruised. But beyond that and her rumpled clothes, she was fine. Ten fingers, ten toes, two arms, two legs. Every limb responded.

To her right, she felt a cool breeze as Helmut opened his car door and jumped out. She pushed herself up onto the seat and began brushing the dirt off of her skirt as her door swung open.

"Are you all right?" How did Helmut make it around the car that fast? His voice was tight and rough, and he reached out a hand toward her.

"Fine. Good thing we weren't moving that fast." She accepted his help out of the car. Her knees were shakier than she'd expected, and he caught her as she trembled. His fingers felt like ice, but his grip on her hand was strong and secure.

"I don't think we were moving at all. The cab was rear-ended." Helmut motioned toward the back where their cab driver was engaged in a fast-flying conversation with what she presumed was the driver of the other car. With her rudimentary French, she couldn't understand a word, but both men gesticulated angrily.

"Let's get off the street." Helmut led her up toward the sidewalk and leaned back against a lamppost. He quietly pulled her toward him and wrapped his arms around her shoulders so that her back was snug tight to his chest. Claire shivered and snuggled in closer. It felt so good to have his strength behind her.

"Are you hurt at all?" she asked belatedly.

"I'm fine. The police should be here soon to take a report." He stood so still, every inch of him solid steel. His breath sounded controlled, though his heart thudded loud and fast in Claire's ears.

She pulled against his arms so she could turn around to face him. The swirl of emotions in his gray green eyes reminded her of the Illinois sky before a tornado.

His mouth closed over hers, his hands pulling her up hard against his chest. She kissed him back, relishing the pure masculine possessiveness of it. Against his molten heat, her nipples hardened, and her panties grew wet with wanting. His hands pulled her buttocks tight against his erection then lifted her to grind her pelvis against his.

Claire almost didn't hear the polite, "Mademoiselle, monsieur, si vous plais."

She pulled her head back, her cheeks flaming as she realized that a police officer stood next to them, pad of paper in hand. Helmut didn't release his hold on her, but his arms did loosen enough for her to turn around. Claire gritted her teeth in annoyance, though she could still feel his hard cock pressing insistently against the swell of her buttocks.

Their report was brief, and in no time they were seated in the back of another, nearly identical cab to the wrinkled one that was now hitched to the back of a tow truck. Helmut kept one arm firmly around Claire's shoulders, while his other hand gripped the door with white-knuckles.

"Helmut," she said, wriggling out of his grasp again. "You okay?"

"I want out of this damned cab." He closed his eyes and sucked in his breath as another car cut in front of the cab and their driver stepped on the brakes quickly.

Claire was also ready to be back at the hotel. She wanted to change clothes, and toss the snagged pantyhose. She had a conference call and a luncheon, and Steph should be calling soon, hopefully with an update on those threatening emails. This afternoon there was a press conference about the Shadow Fly demo tomorrow, and she wanted to go over all of the details with the project manager and the rest of the team.

She watched as Helmut unrolled the window and then rolled it back up again. For a man who was always smiling and joking, it was disconcerting to see him so quiet. And beyond the death grip he maintained on her hand, he didn't say another word until after they stepped out the elevator in the hallway that led to their rooms.

Claire inserted her keycard into the lock, and Helmut pushed the door open for her. She opened her mouth to tell him she'd see him later, but he was already inside. As the door slammed ungracefully behind her, he backed her up against the wall and kissed her again. This kiss was just as demanding as the one on the street corner, and she was soon breathless.

His single-minded focus on her set her reeling, and soon she was breathless. He trailed hot kisses down her neck while his hands scooped up under the hem of her skirt and found the waistband of her hose and her panties. With an efficient yank, she was bare from the waist down, and he lifted her legs up and around his waist and pressed her back against the wall. While she worked on the buttons of his tailored dress shirt, her hands clumsy in her haste to find his smooth, hot flesh.

He pressed a hand into her slick folds, his thumb working her clit and she cried out and clenched around him. Then his cock was inside her, thrusting hard and fast while one hand gently cushioned her head from the wall.

Claire felt like Dorothy from the Wizard of Oz, spinning inside a twister of desire, possession, and other emotions that she couldn't name. Her climax rippled around her in shimmering waves, and Helmut gave a thrust and she felt him shudder inside her.

They clung together for a long moment, their breath slowing, and then gently he eased himself out of her and lowered her legs to the floor.

He looked her in the eyes then, and gently stroked her cheek. He kissed her softly, tenderly, and deeply. And then he quietly walked out, shutting her door softly behind him.

Scalding hot water from the shower washed over Helmut, and steam curled around the marble-tiled shower, rising in innocent white fluffs.

The rush of water and the din of the fan were not loud enough to drown out the screeching of tires and the crunching of metal that played over and over again in his head. His heart had frozen when he'd seen Claire crumpled on the floor of that cab.

No, his heart had frozen thirteen years ago on a dingy stretch of I-55 outside Midway Airport. The towering smokestacks from refineries had been the sole witnesses of the stupidest risk Helmut had ever taken. Today's fender-bender was nothing compared to the twisted heap that had been his Mustang that night.

He closed his eyes as the water poured over his face, stinging eyes that had waited more than a third of his life to cry.

Olivia.

Sweet and full of laughter, with the sultry voice of a fallen angel. His fiancée.

She had died that night because of him. Helmut had wished for years afterwards that he had, too. He had prayed for it. There was no mountain too high, no motorcycle too fast, no gamble too risky for him.

In between his daring escapades, there was work and more work. He had no one to go home to, no wife, no kids. No reason not to put in ninety or more hours a week. The day that should have been his wedding day, he was promoted to department manager.

When his dad died, his mom begged him to come back home to Florida, but he just couldn't see leaving Sheffield & Fox. The company would fall apart without him, he told everyone. He was indispensable.

Helmut sank down onto the floor of the shower, cradling his throbbing head in his hands. The steaming water began to cool as the hotel water heater gave up on him.

He had started dating again, eventually. Ever faster cars and indulgent weekend getaways made him popular. The first time a woman he barely knew said that she loved him, he panicked, and never called again. Women apparently loved a challenge. Knowing he'd screwed and then screwed over one of their own seemed to make him all the more attractive to the rest.

All of them except for Claire.

Teeth chattering, Helmut shut off the water and reached for a towel.

Claire was the first woman in many who didn't chase him, didn't cling, didn't beg. She challenged him, fired him, and shunted him into a tiny private corner of her life. Seeing her proud form humbled by the accident, Helmut knew he'd met his match. Before he left for Paris, he thought he'd already lost everything he cared about. But he hadn't realized he had a heart left to wager.

He wrapped a towel loosely around his waist and stared at himself in the mirror. Did he dare risk what was left of that for Claire?

He needed some fresh air. Or to hit something.

He changed into workout clothes and headed down toward the exercise room. If he was lucky, they'd have some friggin' heavy free weights he could heft until his arms and legs turned to jelly. With his luck of late, he'd be stuck with a treadmill and a yoga mat.

He didn't get that far. The exercise room was off the main lobby, down a side hall past the bar. Tossing back a shot glass at the polished mahogany and chrome counter stood Ben.

"Little early for the hard stuff," Helmut said as he swung a leg over the stool next to Ben's. "Early celebration?"

"What the hell are you doing here, Helmut?"

Helmut signaled the waiter and ordered a glass of water. "Thought I'd go for a jog, but you looked like you needed company. Is that vodka?"

Ben shrugged and poured himself another. And downed it in a single gulp like the first shot.

Helmut grabbed the bottle and pretended to study the label. "That looks like actual Russian. How much does a bottle like this go for, anyway?"

"Don't care. Charged it to the room." Ben wiped his mouth with a cocktail napkin and fixed Helmut with a nasty stare. "What happened, Helmut? Did you forget you got fired and show up for work anyway?"

Helmut casually set the bottle down on his other side. "I thought a vacation was in order, to celebrate my retirement."

Ben snorted. "You? Retire? That'll be the day. I get it. You decided to chase a little CEO skirt and thought you could wine and dine her in Par-ee. Pathetic, man. Flying all this way to win a piddly little bet."

Helmut flushed, but Ben continued without seeming to notice.

"High and mighty a week ago. Now look at you, man. Washed up. Wearing...what the hell are you wearing?"

"Sweats. How much of that bottle did you drink, Ben?"

"Not nearly enough, Helmut, buddy. Not nearly enough." Ben pushed back his barstool and got unsteadily to his feet. "Tell you what, Helmut. I've got a little...something I'm working on. Maybe you can get a piece of it, too. Never let it be said that I don't take care of my friends."

Ben clapped Helmut on the back and wandered out of the bar. Helmut eyed the bottle.

"Is monsieur a friend of yours?" the bartender asked.

"Used to be," Helmut said as he stretched and started to leave.

"The bottle, monsieur. It is paid for. Do you want it?" The young man produced a lid and screwed it back on.

"Thanks," Helmut said. Maybe he could share it with Claire tonight. By the sound of it, it was her money that paid for it.

Chapter 16

Claire punched the off key on her cell phone and glared at the small screen as though it might apologize for Ben. The Shadow Fly project manager was late for his own press conference. Behind her, her VP of marketing flipped through charts on his laptop, preparing to read the presentation cold.

She set the phone down on the folding table in front of her, reached for her bottle of water and took a gulp. Then she glanced at her watch again. And picked up her phone again.

Steph answered on the first ring. "What's wrong, Claire? Why aren't you in the conference room yet?"

"Lackey's MIA."

"Huh. Did someone call his cell?"

Claire let out a breath. So much for Steph's miracles. She should have smuggled the woman into France in her suitcase. "Goes straight to voice mail."

"Huh."

"Is that the best you can do?"

"Chill, Claire, I'm dialing the hotel on the other line as we speak. Hang on."

Claire barely heard Steph's voice in the background, and made out the words "Lackey" and "page," but nothing coherent.

"No answer in his room either. I've got another idea. How long do you have?" Steph asked.

Claire glanced at her watch. "Five minutes. No, four. If you find him before I do, let him know that I'm disappointed that he couldn't join us. No, on second thought, I'm not disappointed."

Steph chuckled. Claire thought she heard a muffled "thanks" as Steph talked to someone on the other phone.

"I called Forrester," Steph said.

"Helmut? Why?" It was a good thing that Steph couldn't see the heat that crept into Claire's cheeks over the phone.

"They're friends, and I know he's in Paris," Steph continued. "He says that he last saw Ben over an hour ago at the hotel. Can you guys handle the presentation?"

"Most of it. But I don't have a single tech person here, and I know a couple of the trade magazines are going to press for details about the engine streamlining we did. I don't have the foggiest idea what that even means."

Steph chuckled again. "I think it means they made it smaller and more efficient. But that's where my knowledge ends. There were a couple of engineers booked for the trip. Go start the press conference and I'll see if I can send them over to answer questions at the end."

"Thanks, Steph. You're a life saver."

The door to the tiny sitting room opened and a slight man wearing a conference coordinator badge waved them out into the hallway. Claire deliberately set a measured pace down the hall, knowing that the other three execs would slow down to let her enter first. No matter how hectic things are backstage, never let your audience see you nervous or they'll eat you alive.

The conference press room was standard issue with half a dozen rows of chairs facing a blue-skirted table lined with microphones. To Claire's surprise, the room was packed. Bright lights flashed as she and her team took their seats at the table and the marketing VP walked to the podium to begin the presentation.

The intro music started up and images of airplanes and American flags began flashing on the video screen behind Claire, and the camera lenses kept on flashing. There were also half a dozen TV cameras running. Claire blinked through the blind spots in her vision and tried to make out the station names. She recognized some major players. NBC, CBS, BBC. Why were the major networks so interested in a remote-controlled helicopter?

The door Claire and the executives had just walked through opened, and Ben Lackey slunk through, closing it quietly behind him. He took an empty chair at the end of the table. With the lights dimmed for the A/V, Claire couldn't see a lot of details, though his hair looked slightly mussed in the front, and his tie had been loosened.

She quickly scribbled Ben's here on a note pad and handed it down the line of chairs toward the podium.

The VP of Marketing managed to introduce Ben so smoothly, it looked like a planned handover. Claire breathed a sigh of relief as Lackey launched into an animated discussion of Shadow Fly. She spent the time surreptitiously studying the audience, and got good vibes. Not too much fidgeting, no one leaving during the presentation. In fact, by the end, they all seemed to hover on the edge of their seats as if waiting for a grand finale.

And then the questions began.

The first two were innocuous enough. Technical details about wing composition and fuel components. Question number three came from one of the major news networks in the back.

"Does Sheffield and Fox have a statement about the Forrester affair?" Claire couldn't make out the face of the reporter through the tangle of cameras and heads.

Ben shot her a glance, and she stood, suppressing a sigh. With a confident smile, she walked to the microphone at the podium and squinted into the bright lights of the projector, which still illuminated the backdrop with the S&F logo and the Shadow Fly photos.

"Good afternoon, everyone. As you probably know, I am Claire Sheffield, CEO of Sheffield and Fox." Cameras flashed, and Claire had to fight to keep from cringing in the assault on her eyes. Her heart constricted as she formed her words carefully.

"In answer to the question about the Forrester affair, I would like to refer you to the press release that we sent out at the beginning of the week. We are still investigating the incident internally, and have begun a massive educational campaign within the company regarding business ethics."

More hands went up. Claire nodded at a woman in the second row.

"Ms. Sheffield, have you forgiven Helmut Forrester?"

Claire frowned at the odd choice of words. "I don't believe that it is my place to either judge or forgive him. This is a business matter, and a legal one."

"Is it true that you fired him?" the woman asked, without waiting for permission.

"The entire board of directors and the executive team, including Mr. Forrester, agreed that it would be best for the investigation and for the company if he sought employment elsewhere for the time being." Claire scanned the room looking for someone else to call on, but every hand had disappeared except for the same woman.

"Ms. Sheffield, would you agree that it is important for a 'twenty-first century company and all of its representatives to avoid even the appearance of impropriety in all business dealings'?"

Claire smiled tightly and clamped down the fear that was fluttering around in her belly. The woman was driving at something. "That sounds like a direct quote from our press release."

"Yes, Ms. Sheffield. It is. Do you consider your current relationship with Mr. Forrester to be 'avoiding the appearance of impropriety'?"

Claire folded her hands together on the podium to keep them from shaking. "I am afraid I don't understand the question."

"Are you romantically involved with Helmut Forrester, Ms. Sheffield?"

Claire took a small, steadying breath. "We move in the same social and business circles. Mr. Forrester worked for many years in the aerospace industry, and for my father. It is inevitable that our paths should cross."

Claire was sure she heard a snort of laughter, but it was quickly muffled. Her cell phone vibrated softly in her jacket pocket, and she silenced it.

"Does anyone have any additional questions about the Shadow Fly project?"

Another hand went up. A man this time, front row center. Close enough for Claire to read his press badge. NBC news. The big guns.

"What is your reaction to the photographs that were posted on the Internet this afternoon, Ms. Sheffield?"

She smiled. "We have tried hard to keep the project under wraps, but there are always leaks. Tomorrow at the live demonstration, you will be able to shoot your own footage, Mr. — "

"The photos aren't of the helicopter. They're of you and Helmut Forrester, taken on a Paris street corner this morning. How 'proper' does it 'appear' to have one of your former employees running his hands up your skirt?"

Helmut clicked off the TV and pulled out his buzzing cell phone. Another text message. The fourteenth in less than five minutes. At this rate, he might actually rival his baby sister's texting records. He rubbed his shoulder and neck, wondering if it was whiplash or stress that made his muscle burn.

Someone had shot a dozen bad photos of him kissing Claire after the car wreck this afternoon. Close-up shots, but not great resolution. If he ever met the inventor of the camera phone, he'd throttle the son of a bitch. His phone had been buzzing constantly since they hit the presses half an hour ago.

This message was from Betty, asking him to call her. He wondered if she had seen the photos and was calling to yell at him. Or if she had a lead on Claire's threatening emails.

All of the news networks were flashing close-ups of his hand on Claire's ass and repeating snippets of the damned press release from last week's story. His affair with Juliana and the contract scandal had been a tiny blurb buried six pages deep in the business section. With this afternoon's photos, he'd just landed on the front page.

He had to talk to Claire. See how she was dealing with the photos.

Had his world really turned upside down in thirty minutes?

He'd had no trouble finding footage of the press conference on the web. The tiny video wasn't much better than the photos, and the shadows from the projector had made it hard to read Claire's facial expression. But he knew that set of her shoulders. And the clipped tones she'd used to abruptly end the questions and leave the room.

Helmut hit redial on his phone.

"What's up, Betty?" He held his breath, ready for the verbal lashing.

"I found your HAF," she said. No word about the photos. He wondered if Betty would follow him to Italy. He wondered if Italy would still be a possibility after this afternoon's disaster.

"Her name is Harriet Freeman, and she's an expert in thermodynamics. She works—worked—in one of the test labs. Her work record is spotless. And her report on the most recent set of structural tests was frightening."

Helmut sat down as Betty read excerpts from it.

"Catastrophic failure" and "Highly explosive nature." and "Structural Faults."

"Betty, what do you know about this woman? Is this for real?"

She hesitated. "I'm not an engineer, Helmut. But this is what worries me. She forwarded me emails that she sent to Ben over the past few weeks, warning him about her lab findings. She has his responses, too—he told her to test it again. And when she got similar results a second time, he assigned someone else to the project. She holds a PhD in this area, and her replacement was a lab tech with an associate's degree from a technical college."

Helmut sat quietly as the words sank in.

"Helmut, I know Ben is a friend of yours. But is it possible that he has made a bad judgment here?"

Helmut closed his eyes and images flashed across his eyelids. Squealing tires. A sickening crunch of metal. Smoke. Too much smoke. Flashing lights and sirens. A black sheet covering an ambulance stretcher. He opened them and forced himself to look around. This was a hotel room, not a dark stretch of highway. He couldn't take a chance with another life. Not Claire's.

"Betty, can you get the woman to Paris by morning?" he asked. "I don't care what it costs. Do you still have my credit card number? And tell her to bring a copy of every email and lab report she's got."

"I'll see what I can do, Helmut," she said. "I'll let you know when I get her on a flight."

Helmut clicked off the phone and clicked on the TV. One of the satellite channels was airing the major network news. There on the screen stood James Sheffield, surrounded by microphones with his wife, Diana, tugging on one sleeve. The reporters fired questions from all sides at once, all variations of a theme.

"What do you think of Claire's relations with Helmut Forrester?"

"Are you aware that the Air Force is now investigating the legalities of your Shadow Fly contract?"

"Why did you really appoint your daughter as CEO? Do you still run Sheffield and Fox?"

"How do you feel about your daughter having a relationship with a known philanderer like Forrester?"

Helmut sat on the edge of the bed, elbows on his knees, resting his forehead on his hands. What would the man say about his treatment of Claire? What would Helmut do if Claire were his daughter? He pictured his sister sitting abandoned in that restaurant, no money, no cell phone, no transportation. Screwed over by some asshole of a boyfriend.

If he were James, Helmut would beat himself black and blue.

"Ladies and Gentlemen," James began, holding up one hand to silence the rapid-fire questions. Once he had the attention of the reporters who surrounded him, he looked straight into the camera. "I have a statement. But I am not speaking as the Chairman of the Board of S&F. An official spokesperson will issue a statement soon."

A roar of complaints went up from the waiting press. James held up one hand again and the rumble of voices quieted again. "I have a statement as Claire Sheffield's father. Claire is my youngest child, and my only daughter. As all fathers are, I suspect, I feel very protective toward her. She may not always believe that of me. Lord knows I've made enough mistakes of my own.

"And I have known Helmut Forrester for many years," James continued. "Though Claire will always be my little girl, my daughter is a full grown woman who makes her own decisions. She could do far worse than to engage in a relationship with Forrester. For Helmut, he could not find anyone better. Now, butt out of my family's private lives and return to covering legitimate news stories."

Helmut stared at the TV as the news anchors began making polite speculation as to the company's official reaction to the scandal would be.

James had just stuck up for him. It wasn't a ringing endorsement, but the man could have lambasted Helmut for all the world to hear. It was something.

Claire shut herself into her hotel room, where it was quiet at last.

Her neck ached, and her knee, where it had banged against the divider wall in the cab. She stood up and walked to the bathroom, the salty tears making her contacts burn. She took ibuprofen and then had to practically chisel the lenses off her eyeballs. She slipped on her glasses — narrow, thick-framed, ones she thought made her look scholarly.

She had a message from Helmut. "Call me back. It's urgent."

With a sniff, she padded back to the bedroom. As she exchanged her ruined suit for a pair of yoga pants and a tank top, she tried to remember what her plans for the evening were supposed to be. Oh yeah, a casual interview over coffee with one of the reporters from Business Week. Not doing that now.

She contemplated her cell phone. Helmut was supposed to be a casual fling. A nice little indulgent interlude with a man used to casual flings and indulgent interludes. He was like a chocolate truffle. Delicious, but not something she could eat for dinner every night. So how had she let her body come to crave his touch, long for his arms to hold and comfort her? When did she begin to crave his smile, his wry sense of humor?

He was probably just down the hall. She shivered, remembering him pressing her up against the hotel door just that afternoon. How easily she had surrendered to that passion, without a single thought for what was in her best interest. Her career's best interest. Her company's best interest.

She needed to clear her head. She deleted the voice mail. She would talk to him tomorrow.

She found her cell phone and texted Steph, asking her to cancel the Business Week interview. Claire had the reporter's cell phone number, but she didn't trust her own voice.

"Way ahead of you," came the text reply not two minutes later. "Pls call."

Claire dialed.

Steph picked right up. "You can totally salvage this, Claire. Any press is good press, right? At least you've guaranteed that the stands will be filled for tomorrow's demo flight. Nothing like a little sex scandal to get butts in the seats."

"Is that all you've got? I'm such an idiot, Steph." Claire sat down in the office chair at the small computer desk and spun lightly back and forth. "What is it with my taste in men?"

"Didn't you tell me you were going into this one with your eyes wide open?"

Claire caught herself mid-spin. "Well, yes, but I thought...I don't know what I thought."

"He is a major improvement over Frank."

Claire heard clicking noises coming from the background.

"Oh, shit, Claire."

"What now?"

"Your father. He just made a statement."

Suddenly the two lamps in the room were too much light. Claire squeezed her eyes shut against the drilling pain that shot through her skull. "Don't tell me, Steph. I'm going to sleep."

"It could be a lot worse, Claire. Do you even want to know what he said?"

Claire pictured her father's stern face when she'd told him about Frank's cheating earlier that day. "Not particularly. Talk to you in the morning."

Chapter 17

Hotel room service delivered the worst-tasting fifteen dollar cup of coffee Claire had ever had. She winced as she took a hearty gulp, hoping that "bad" meant "full of caffeine." She would need every milligram to stay on her game through this morning's demo. Just a few more hours and she could catch a plane home. Away from the reporters. Away from the mess she had made.

She unwrapped the towel from her freshly-shampooed hair and sat down at the desk, comb in hand, and flipped open her laptop. While it booted, she focused on the tangles in her hair, and tried to breathe deeply and slowly. Too bad she couldn't fix the knot in her stomach with a comb.

Steph was a miracle worker. Claire had turned over control of her email inbox last week to monitor and sort the contents. Steph must have been up half the night keeping tabs on the incoming messages. There were only a dozen entries on the main screen, each of them work-related. Claire deliberately ignored the brand-new folders labeled "Interview Requests," "Well-wishers," and "Handle At Home."

Leaving her hair to air-dry, Claire began at the top of the list of actual work. First, a memo from accounting. The corporate credit-card snafu had been cleared up, and the card company had mailed replacement cards to everyone. Next was a summary of industry news clips for the day, including details on a new luxury jet model being released by one of S&F's competitors that would compete directly with several of their own models. One of the technical managers had a report on how new FAA guidelines regarding radio usage in flight would affect the production lines next year.

At the bottom of the list was the weekly profit-and-loss report of all of the business units, auto-generated out of the accounting system every Friday night. The numbers were always raw, and sometimes had errors or missing entries. But Claire liked to see the data that way. Even in-flux, the numbers gave her a good sense of how things were really going.

She broke off a chunk of the brittle croissant that had accompanied her coffee, and began skimming the columns. One number stood out. A huge expense check, over fifty thousand dollars, just cleared two days ago for the Shadow Fly project. At least two executives had to sign off on a single payout that large, and she had no idea what it could be for. Claire clicked on the number to see a digital copy of the expense report, and saw an error message instead. "Network Communication Failure." She tried several other fields in the report. All had the same problem.

Claire dialed Steph immediately.

"What's wrong?" her friend said sleepily.

"Sorry to wake you, Steph. I was looking at the Friday P-n-L. I wanted to drill into some of the numbers, but I can't get to any of the detail reports. What's with that?"

Steph yawned into the phone. "I saw that last week, too. When I asked someone in IT, they said the links only work when we're on our network in the office. Tell me which ones you need, and I'll email them to you separately."

Claire glanced at her watch. It was three a.m. in Chicago. "Thanks, but I'll be home by tomorrow night. It can wait until then. I don't need you cabbing all over town this time of night just for a few numbers."

Steph mumbled something incoherent, and Claire said goodbye. She could ask Ben Lackey about the charge at the demo soon enough.

She dressed carefully, choosing the most conservative black pantsuit left in her garment bag. The fabric was heavy for the late spring day, but she wanted to look as polished and austere as possible. The photo image of herself, blond hair tumbling loose over her shoulders and skirt hitched up to her thighs was not something she wanted reinforced with the press. S&F's luxury planes should be sexy, not its executives.

Clutching her laptop case tightly in both hands, Claire stepped into the hallway and paused for only the briefest moment before lifting her chin and walking toward the elevator. She ignored the thudding of her heart and the lump in her throat as she walked past Helmut's door. She wondered whether he was on the other side of it, watching the news, or sleeping. He could have company for all she knew.

Matt, the Marketing VP, met her in the hotel lobby. He greeted Claire politely enough, but the ride to the airport was silent torture. She could feel his unasked questions clouding the air in the town car, like smoke in a crowded bar.

She had no answers to give him.

There was no point in jumping to a defense. That would only make her look guilty of something. As for any other discussion of her relationship with Helmut, well, she had to discuss that with Helmut first.

Relationship.

Claire turned the word over and over in her mind, like a puzzle she couldn't quite solve. Was this a relationship? It was sex, definitely. She didn't want any more than that. Did she? She'd had a relationship with Frank for years. One full of humiliation and dependency. And sex. And a few fun memories, especially early on. And lots of humdrum ones. Did she really want to face that again?

Helmut was fun. He was exciting. He was worth having shaved legs and sexy underwear, witty stories culled from the week's doldrums of work so she could make him smile. He was shiny and new and mysterious. A relationship meant stubble and morning breath and showing her granny panties and ratty old bathrobe. Conversations about groceries and laundry and unloading the day's struggles on sympathetic ears. It was seeing his toothbrush next to hers in the bathroom, and his feet propped next to hers on the coffee table.

She had to cut off this train of thought right there, before the image of the two of them cuddled on the couch, watching the evening news started sounding good. Way too damn good. Claire stared out the window as the scenery changed from cityscape to industrial as they neared the airport.

Matt finally broke the silence. "Have you talked to Lackey this morning?"

"No. He's supposed to get there early with the aircrew and technical support team, setting up."

"Yeah, well, I hope the guy got some sleep last night. I gather some of the team was out late working."

Claire frowned. She had meant to go over today's briefing with Lackey after the press conference yesterday, but got derailed by the scandal. As soon as they'd gotten off the stage, she'd jumped in a cab for the hotel.

The cab driver had to drop them at the security checkpoint. They flashed their conference ID badges and caught a lift on a courtesy golf cart to the hangar where the S&F team was setting up.

Inside the metal-sheathed building, one of the company's private jets, used for transporting the technical team and all of their equipment, was parked. Most of the wide concrete floor was left open, with a row of steel workbenches arranged along one wall.

It reminded Claire a bit of a woodworker's shop, with power tools scattered across the lengths of countertop. On closer inspection, it was more of a mad inventor's basement. Scraps of metal and piles of screws, fasteners, and bundles of cable lay here and there. Off to one side was a metal divider with a welder's mask propped up against it.

Lackey was there, huddled with two other employees she had only briefly met, looking at a computer screen with what she thought was a schematic drawing of the tiny helicopter that they'd be demonstrating today. One of the men gestured at the screen while Lackey shook his head.

He glanced her way and straightened. Grabbing his suit jacket from the workbench behind him, he crossed the ten yards of concrete floor at half a run. "Good morning, Ms., er, Claire. Can I get you a cup of coffee?"

He took her by the elbow and steered her away from the workers.

"Uh, thanks, Lackey. I wouldn't mind meeting your team when they have a minute," she said as she followed him toward a kitchenette. "I wanted to review the agenda for this morning's presentation, and I have a couple of questions on this week's p-n-l."

"Great, great." He glanced over his shoulder and shut the door behind them. The kitchen space wasn't much more than a sink, a mini fridge, and a microwave with a small laminate table along the opposite wall. Not luxurious, but there was a tray of bagels and pastries and a large carafe of hot coffee and paper cups.

"I hear you had a late night last night," she asked as he fussed over choosing a paper plate and a napkin. While he worked, Claire studied the man. He was good enough looking, she supposed, with sandy brown hair that looked ruffled above one temple, and clean-cut features. He handed over a cup of steaming black coffee, and she could see dark circles under his eyes.

"No biggie," he said with an exaggeratedly relaxed shrug. "Just the usual cram session. Guess I never broke the habit from college. What did you want to go over?"

With the table full of pastries, there was no room to set anything down. Claire handed him back the coffee and pulled out a copy of the expense report she'd printed before she left this morning.

"Check these out," she said as she exchanged her papers for the coffee.

"What the—" Ben ran his free hand through his hair as he skimmed his eyes over the numbers.

The door opened, and a young woman in khakis and a Sheffield & Fox golf shirt stuck her head in. "Ben, we need a decision on the—"

He cut her off. "Coming." Ben shrugged helplessly and shot Claire what she supposed passed for a charming grin. "Forgive me, Ms. Sheffield. Duty calls. Terry can walk you out to the tent by the bleachers. We have chairs set up, and a table if you needed to spread out your work. I'll come by as soon as I can."

Claire caught the quelling glance he tossed at Terry as he passed her out of the kitchen, and she frowned again, wondering what was going on.

The woman, Terry, wasn't much help. Claire asked her a few polite questions about her job and how long she'd been with the company, but got the barest answers imaginable.

Matt was already waiting under the shade of the canopy, talking on his cell phone, laptop open in front of him. Claire settled in and flipped open her own.

Helmut gripped the passenger handle of the cab with all of his strength. The driver was erratic, stopping suddenly and speeding up too quickly, throwing them around the passenger seat. Harriet Freeman sat next to him, staring open-eyed outside the car windows.

She was exactly what he had expected from an engineer: somewhat mousy, with a plain face and dull brown hair, and average figure. But her eyes sparkled with intelligence and she had an air of open honesty about her.

"Have you ever been to Paris before?" he asked, flinching as the cabbie slammed on his brakes again.

"No. Will we pass the city?"

"Le Bourget is only a few miles down the road from the main commercial airport. We would probably already be there if it weren't for all of the traffic."

"Oh." Her face fell.

"You can do some sightseeing later."

"Maybe. I wish my husband could have come with me. We talked about Paris for our honeymoon, but decided on a cruise instead. Maybe for our ten-year anniversary next year. It's supposed to be such a romantic city."

Helmut smiled tightly. Romantic indeed.

His ID got them in the gate of the show, but not through the VIP gate. The cabbie left them by the entrance. Helmut glanced at his watch then at the exhibition map posted by the entrance. "The demo starts in half an hour, but it's on the far side. You OK to walk?"

"No problem," she said with a half-smile. Harriet hitched a laptop bag over one shoulder and followed Helmut, wheeling a small carry-on suitcase behind her.

They passed through exhibition halls and crowded corridors, weaving around throngs of people crowded around a display of airplane seats showcasing built-in entertainment screens.

"Mr. Forrester," his companion said. "I was wondering about something."

Helmut's footsteps slowed. Her face was red, and she seemed to be struggling with keeping the laptop bag balanced on one shoulder. Helmut gently took the suitcase from her. "Call me Helmut. What were you wondering?"

"Why did you believe me, when Lackey didn't? Everyone knows...I mean, I thought that I heard..." Her face blushed a deeper shade of red.

"That we were buddies?"

She nodded.

Helmut clenched his jaw. "Some things are more important than your buddies."

She nodded again, and seemed satisfied with his answer.

"What about you, Harriet? Why was this so important to you? Assuming you're right—and I do believe you—you are risking an awful lot by this. Your job for one."

She shrugged. "Some things are more important than jobs."

Helmut's lips quirked. Two weeks ago, he thought nothing was more important than work. But his job was long gone. By interrupting a press conference, he risked Claire's anger, and her company's reputation. By not interrupting, he risked her life. He picked up the pace, making sure Harriet kept up with him.

After the long walk through the interior of the show, the bright sun blinded Helmut. And a security guard stopped him at the ropes leading to the bleachers.

"Your pass, sir?" the man asked in heavily accented English. He a thin patch of salt and pepper hair ringing a shiny bald spot that glared like a headlight in the morning light.

Helmut flashed his ID.

"And the mademoiselle?"

Helmut glanced at his watch. They only had about ten minutes left before the conference was set to start. "Can't I bring her in as my guest?" he asked.

"No, monsieur. Everyone must have a pass."

"Mr. Forrester, maybe I should wait here?" asked Harriet, shading her eyes with one hand.

"There's not enough time." Helmut turned back to the guard. "Check your guest list. The name's Forrester. Helmut Forrester."

The guard all but rolled his eyes and began flipping through a sheaf of papers.

Helmut tapped his fingers against the side of his leg as the man slowly examined every page of the list.

Finally he raised both hands apologetically. "No, monsieur. You are not on the list. With your ID badge, you may sit in general admission. Mademoiselle will need to purchase a ticket."

Helmut glanced inside past the ropes. The bleachers sat on the far side of the tarmac from the stage and podium. Beyond that he saw a white canvas tent with one flap folded back. He thought he recognized Matt from Marketing talking on his cell phone.

This has to work.

"Thanks," he muttered to the guard, and steered Harriet away from the gate and into the shade of an information sign. He pulled out his cell phone and dialed, his eyes on the tent in the distance.

Claire didn't answer.

"Ladies and Gentlemen, please take your seats," announced a loudspeaker in English, and followed it with a trill of French and Italian.

Shit. Shit. He was out of time.

"Look, Harriet," Helmut started. "Maybe I should just go in myself, and..."

She wasn't listening, he saw. She was on her own cell phone, waiving her arms toward the entrance. "We're in," she said as she hung up. "Come on."

She hurried off around the side of the show area.

"What did you do?" he asked as he followed her.

"Friends," she said simply as they came up to a side entrance. A woman in khakis and a Sheffield and Fox golf shirt waited for them.

"Harriet, what are you doing here?" the other woman said.

"How is the shell holding up, Terry? Are there any more of the cracks around the motor?" Harriet asked as a security guard waved them through. This time Helmut had to hurry to catch up to the women.

They shot questions back and forth, and Helmut was quickly out of his depth in the technical jargon.

"You can't let that thing lift off, Anne," Harriet said. "If you're already seeing the stress marks on the hull, then there's too much heat."

"I tried to tell Lackey. He wants to go ahead. Thinks the risks are small," Anne said.

"Where is Claire?" Helmut interrupted.

"Claire Sheffield?" Anne asked. "She was in the tent a few minutes ago. Oh no, they're starting."

Twenty yards ahead of him, Helmut spotted Claire. She was taking her place on a chair up on the stage, and Ben stood behind the podium. The intro music started, and cheers went up from the crowd as two men in fatigues walked out to the concrete pad in the center, carrying the small helicopter.

Anne pulled out a small walkie-talkie, but Helmut didn't listen to what she said. He took off at a sprint toward the stage. He climbed the steps three at a time and hurried over to the empty chair next to Claire's.

"What are you doing here?" she hissed at him under her breath.

"Claire, you have to stop the demo." The music picked up as images of airplanes and American flags flashed on a jumbo screen beside the stage.

"What?"

"Stop the demo. Now. That thing's not safe." He had to speak up to be heard over the noise as the opening video started.

"I can't," she said. "We've already started."

Helmut felt a tap on his shoulder. "I think you're in my seat, Helmut," he said. Ben's eyes flashed angrily and Helmut recognized something else. Fear.

"Call it off, Ben. Now, before someone gets hurt. I brought Harriet—"

"That woman's crazy. Claire, get rid of him. Hasn't he embarrassed you enough?"

Helmut searched Claire's eyes. Her gaze flickered between the two men.

"Claire, I found your HAF. She's an engineer who works for you. And she thinks that helicopter is dangerous. Cancel the demo."

"I'll get security." Ben made to leave. "What are you doing here?"

Harriet rushed up onto the stage. "Ms. Sheffield. Shadow Fly is not safe. Cancel it, now. Terry already tried, and they don't have their radios on."

At the purr of a motor, Helmut glanced up. Six-foot long blades began whirring as the two operators backed away from the small spy helicopter.

"Who are y—" Claire began to ask, her eyes wide. Helmut grabbed one of her hands. Her fingers felt like ice.

"Security!" Ben yelled.

Harriet ran right past them to the microphone. Ben lunged at her and tried to grab her. "Stop. Halt the demo. Now. Tony and Mark, take it down."

Security guards rushed the stage. One grabbed at Helmut's arm, yanking his grip away from Claire's.

Helmut would have gone quietly with the man. But at the loud pop and the gasp from the crowd, every pair of eyes riveted to the sky, including the guards.

Shadow Fly popped again, and began spinning wildly, falling downward. Aimed at the stage. Helmut didn't think. He shook off the guards' loose grips, grabbed Claire, and dove for the floor cradling her head with his hands and protecting her body with his.

He covered her with his body as the fire exploded somewhere above them, raining debris across the tarmac and the stage. Helmut felt something smash against one of his legs. The smell of smoking grease and screech of emergency sirens sent him spiraling back to I55 and the car crash.

His fiancée had been reaching over the back seat, grabbing for a tape to play her latest composition for him. Helmut had not been paying enough attention to the road, exhausted from travel after a business trip of sixteen-hour days.

In one instant of inattention, he lost control of the car.

He'd lost control of his life. Work was the only thing left to him for years, and he'd let that spiral out of control, too. Until today.

"Helmut," Claire pushed at his chest. Her sea blue eyes were wide, and a smudge of soot streaked one temple. Her heart beat wildly against his.

"Are you all right?" he whispered.

"I think so. You?"

He took stock. Blood thundering in his ears, and his breath felt ragged, but he didn't feel injured. Their torsos were pressed together against the rough carpet of the stage, and he felt a surge of desire as she shifted underneath him, brushing her belly against his cock. He smoothed a stray lock from her mussed hair.

She pushed lightly at him again, and Helmut sat back and let her sit up. Chaos was everywhere. The crowds rushing out of the bleachers. Firefighters spraying foam on the steaming remains of the Shadow Fly helicopter.

"I think everyone's OK," she whispered back.

"Claire." I love you. The words formed on his tongue, but rough arms grabbed him. As security led him away from the scene of the crash, he looked back. Claire walked down the steps from the stage, assisted by another guard.

Chapter 18

The French authorities questioned him. The American authorities questioned him. For six hours, Helmut sat in a featureless white room with only two folding chairs and a chipped laminate table.

He paced the room restlessly, throwing glares at the large mirror on one wall, no doubt a two-way mirror. Information. If they could just tell him whether Claire was OK, and whether anyone in the crowd, Harriet, and the two operators who had been on the tarmac at the time of the explosion were safe and sound.

He answered every question with as much patience as he could muster. It was a thin veneer.

"Why were you at the air show today?" a man in US Air Force fatigues asked. This was the fourth interrogator, and Helmut didn't care to remember the man's name or rank. He just wanted out of the room.

"To warn the Sheffield and Fox team that there was a structural instability in Shadow Fly."

"Did you know the aircraft would explode?" The man asked every question as though he were asking about Helmut's grocery list, and barely looked up from his own notebook.

"Not specifically, no. The engineer, Harriet, had warned me that the hull was weak and had shown problems during lab testing. Her reports had not apparently been taken seriously, so I brought her over here to give them in person." Helmut ran his hand through his hair. "Look, I've told the last three guys the exact same thing. Ask Harriet, or my secretary —"

"Can you explain the weakness in the hull?"

Helmut clenched his jaw and took a calming breath. "No, I can't. I'm an accountant, not an engineer."

The man set down his notepad on the table and looked directly at Helmut for the first time. "I understand that you recently left Sheffield and Fox under less than ideal circumstances."

"Thanks to the media the past two days, I believe all of France knows all about that. Why ask me now?"

"Because it's my job to ask." The man leaned forward and rested his elbows on the table, fixing Helmut with a stare no doubt designed to intimidate new recruits. Helmut returned it, steel for steel. He had nothing to hide.

"Mr. Forrester, were you in any way responsible for the explosion of that helicopter?" the man asked.

Helmut snorted. "If I wanted the thing to blow up, why would I have rushed the stage trying to stop the demonstration?"

Helmut held the other man's gaze. Finally the man nodded. "I'm going to level with you. Both Ms. Sheffield and Ms. Friedman have fully corroborated your story. You might be glad to know that we do not consider you a terrorism suspect."

Helmut started. "Terrorism? What the h-"

"Sir, I realize that this has been a long day, but I am not quite finished with my questions. I need to ask you about Benjamin Lackey."

Helmut jumped to his feet and paced over to the two-way mirror. Terrorism? Ben? No frigging way. He leaned against the wall and crossed his arms over his chest.

"Mr. Forrester, how long have you known Mr. Lackey?"

"Fifteen, no, sixteen years. We both started at S&F on the same day."

"And you maintain a friendly relationship?"

"More or less."

"Are you familiar with Mr. Lackey's financial situation? Does he have gambling debts or drug problems or bankruptcies? Anything of that nature? Under any unusual stress lately?"

Helmut shrugged. He'd always watched his own net worth, and assumed Ben took care of his. "I haven't talked to him much in the past two or three months. I figured he's been swamped by the Shadow Fly project, and I've been a bit distracted. Sure, he gambles some, goes to Vegas once or twice a year, plays cards, nothing to worry about."

The man scratched a few notes onto his paper. "I will leave you my card, Mr. Forrester. If you think of anything else that would help with this matter, please give me a call."

Thermometer under her tongue, Claire tapped her foot impatiently as a nurse with a flighty French accent and dark hair pinned beneath an old-fashioned nursing hat checked Claire's blood pressure. The tight pressure on her left arm eased, and the nurse pulled the plastic-covered probe out of Claire's mouth.

"Normal and normal, Madame."

"Of course it's normal. Bumping your knee on the ground doesn't give you the flu," Claire muttered.

"I am sorry, Madame. What do you say?"

Get me out of here. "Nothing, sorry. Is the doctor busy?" Claire glanced toward the door of the small private room in the American Hospital of Paris where she and a handful of other people from the show had been brought, including the two operators who were on the tarmac when the helicopter exploded.

So far, she had seen a police and an Air Force investigator, the nurse, and a reporter who had slipped past the front desk. And the security guard brought by the nurse to escort out the reporter. But no doctor. Not that she needed one. But no one wanted to let her leave without seeing the elusive medic.

"Oui, madame, the doctor is busy. He will be along shortly." The nurse smiled and scratched a note onto the chart by the door. "You have a gentleman visitor, Madame. Shall I send him in?"

Helmut. "Yes, please." Media reports be damned. The thought of being enfolded in Helmut's arms sounded like pure bliss. Quickly Claire smoothed her hair and her rumpled sleeve.

The door opened and Claire's heart sank. "Frank. What the hell are you doing here?"

He strode in, smiling. "Claire, dear. What a day you've had. How are you?" He stopped in front of the hospital bed where she perched, his arms open wide.

Claire crossed her arms over her chest and glared at him. "I guess I should have asked who my visitor was."

"Expecting someone else?" he asked with a hurt expression on his face.

"Oh don't start with your theatrics, Frank. I'm not in the mood for it. Just go, okay?"

He hooked the small rolling stool with one foot and drew it to him to sit. "Claire, I'm not here to fight with you."

She raised one eyebrow.

"Honestly. I am worried about you. Every time I see you lately, you look stressed and harassed."

"Ever think that perhaps you're the reason for that?" She sounded much sassier than she'd meant to. She was slipping back into old habits with this man. She had to collect herself before she ended up in a shouting match. That would benefit no one.

Frank let out a breath. He had small wrinkles around the sides of his eyes, and a crinkle on his forehead. Those were new. "I deserve that, I suppose. I know I've made a lot of mistakes, Claire, but I do care about you. Can you really look back at ten years and say that I mean nothing to you? We've had a lot of good times together. Surely I deserve another chance."

Claire raised one eyebrow. Good lord, the man actually looked sincere.

He pried one of her hands from where she'd tucked it at her waist and clasped it in his two. They were warm and strong, and he fixed her with the same deep brown eyes that used to make her heart flutter.

In college, Claire had capitalized on her newfound freedom, her father's money, and her blond good looks to pledge the premier sorority, to date the school's hot-shot athletes, to be the ultimate party girl. It was a fun, empty life. Frank was quiet, shy almost. His chocolate eyes had sparkled with intelligence, and he'd been the first to be interested in her brain, not her boobs. She'd fallen hard for him.

Claire let him keep the hand. She sighed. "We did have a lot of fun, Frank. We grew up together in a way."

He gave her hand a little yank, trying to pull her into a hug. The spicy scent of his cologne was so familiar, but today it overwhelmed her nose. She pushed back.

"I appreciate your concern. But I'm not twenty-two any more. I've given you too much energy, too many years. And too many chances already. Move on, Frank."

"Claire, I miss you." He leaned forward and rested his elbows on the edge of the bed. His hands were close to her thighs, and Claire wriggled away.

Once, Claire had been thrilled with the way Frank had clung to her. He thrived on her company, sought out her attentions. And her advice. After years of indifference from her father, and leers from other men, it was intoxicating to be wanted for more than her body. She couldn't remember when the constant need grew old. When she started wanting him to grow a spine of his own. To have his own opinion, and quit leeching on hers.

And when she'd withdrawn, he'd responded by fucking every moderately attractive female in his company.

"I appreciate your worry, Frank. But it's over between us. It has been for a long time now. I've moved on. You should, too."

His eyebrows narrowed and his eyes flashed. "Moved on? You call Helmut Forrester 'moving on?'"

"What I do or don't call Helmut Forrester is none of your business." Claire swung her legs over the opposite side of the bed and strode to the door. She flung it open. The noise and hustle of the hall washed over Claire. "Out. Now."

Frank stood his ground. "I can't believe you're defending a man who's done nothing but take advantage of you. Claire—"

"Conversation over. Out." As he pointed her index finger out into the hall, it struck something warm and soft, and totally unexpected. Ben Lackey's chest.

"Nice to see you again, Burwell. Is this a bad time?" the newcomer asked, looking with amusement from Claire to Frank and back again.

"Yes," said Frank.

"No," said Claire. "Frank here was just leaving."

Ben ran one hand through his already ruffled hair and then over his chin, where Claire could see a faint trace of stubble. His suit from earlier in the day was wrinkled, and his tie gone. "Were you talking about Helmut?"

Clare stammered for a moment, then collected herself. Ben Lackey was known to be friendly with Helmut, though she hadn't failed to notice their hostility this morning. Understandable, given that Helmut had arrived just in time for Lackey's pet project to fall to pieces, along with the remains of her company's reputation.

Besides CNN, Claire couldn't think of anyone she'd like to talk to less right this moment. "This is a personal matter between the two of us. I will touch base with you later, Lackey."

"Sure, sure. I just wanted to let you know what was going on with Helmut."

Claire froze. Was he hurt?

Helmut had shoved her to the ground, covered her body with his while shrapnel rained from the sky. She had been ushered off the tarmac so quickly, she had completely lost track of everyone else. And the damned doctor hadn't released her to go wandering the halls.

"What happened to him?" she asked, her voice wavering.

His lips quirked into a smirk. "Helmut's not hurt. Not yet, anyway. But after those news reports hit yesterday about your affair, I though you should know..."

Claire exhaled. Helmut was not hurt. *Wait, what did he mean by "not yet"?*

"I didn't think it was my place to intrude, you know. Helmut's always been my buddy. But he's really gone off the deep end this time," Ben rambled.

"Get to the point, Lackey," Claire demanded.

He glanced over her shoulder at Frank, who was watching the entire exchange with great interest.

Claire frowned at the two men. "Frank, do you mind?"

"No, not at all. I'm quite enjoying the show. Do go on, Ben."

Ben shrugged his shoulders and gave Claire a sly grin. "Well, like I said, Helmut's always been a friend of mine. I know he was upset about not getting the CEO appointment. And then losing his job... I think the guy is out for revenge against you Claire. He even bet me a thousand bucks he could get you into bed. I tried to talk him out of it..."

Claire felt the air rush out of her lungs. Revenge. A thousand bucks.

Lackey was still talking, but she quit hearing his words. They stopped making any sense. The photos.

Helmut had screwed her over. Professionally. Personally. And she had practically begged him to do it.

She had to get out of here. Now.

She ignored Frank's voice calling her from the exam room as she left. She walked past the nurses' station without saying a word and headed straight for the exit without looking back.

Helmut paced his hotel room for the hundredth time. Claire hadn't been at the police station, and after he'd been released, it had taken half a dozen phone calls before someone told him where she was. The hospital. Holy shit, if she was hurt... He couldn't even finish the thought. He had no idea what he would do.

He headed out of his hotel room and into the elevator. He should be able to catch a cab to the hospital from the lobby. Whether he could talk any of the staff to letting him see her, he didn't care.

The elevator doors opened into the marble and gilt lobby, and Helmut found himself facing Claire's shell-shocked expression.

He drank in the sight of her. Her suit jacket was off, and her hair looked wild. Another woman might look like a victim, but Claire carried off the tousled look like a woman who'd just rolled from his bed.

She recovered first. "Not now, Helmut." Her voice was ice, and she glanced over her shoulder as if expecting an ambush.

He grabbed her by the hand, pulled her back into the elevator, and punched the button for their floor. She struggled lightly against his hand, but he held firm until the shiny gold doors closed on them.

"Let go of me."

Helmut released her hand and she fled to the opposite corner.

"Claire, they told me you were at the hospital. How are you? I've been worried shitless all afternoon."

Her eyes widened and she stared at him, mouth agape. "I sincerely doubt that."

He took a step closer, trying to bridge the gap. His arms itched to hold her and soothe away the fear and chaos of the afternoon.

The elevator stopped on a lower floor and the doors whooshed open. Claire practically jumped out.

Helmut followed, nearly running over a bellhop with a huge round tray laden with empty plates. "Sorry," he said as he helped the young man catch his careening tray. "Claire, wait."

He glanced down the empty hall and saw the door to the stairwell just clicking closed. He ran after her.

Hurried small footsteps echoed from above him. Helmut leaned gently over the rail and looked up. "Claire, can we talk for a moment."

"No. We can't." The footsteps sped up.

Helmut followed, taking the steps two at a time. She was fast, but he had longer legs, and he started gaining right away.

"I'm as pissed by the photos as you are. This isn't exactly going to help my job hunt, you know." He knew he'd passed two floors already, and was beginning to breathe heavily.

"I'm sure you'll think of something."

Helmut swore to himself. He thought he would have gained ground, but she was still a full story above him.

"This will blow over, Claire. I'm not an employee anymore. No one will even remember it by next week."

Her footsteps stopped. Thankfully. Helmut slowed his pace, still taking the steps two at a time, but no longer sprinting them. "Man you're in good shape," he said with a grin.

He climbed another story to where he'd last heard her voice, but she wasn't there. Helmut stopped and rested his palms on his knees, breathing deeply. "Where'd you go, Claire?"

He listened and heard nothing. Wait, not nothing. A soft slapping sound. Damnit, she'd taken off her shoes and continued upwards. Helmut glanced at the door behind him. Eighth floor. Their rooms were on the fourteenth.

He began sprinting in earnest, but he was too late. Just as he passed door number twelve, he heard her leave the stairwell.

A minute later, he pounded on the door to her suite. "I'm not leaving until you answer, Claire."

Silence.

"If I keep yelling like this, someone will call security. Wouldn't you rather avoid another scene?"

Bingo. That got a reaction. Her door cracked, and he went to push it open, but she'd left it chained from the inside.

"Just go away, Helmut. You've done enough." Her voice sounded muffled.

Helmut scanned the inside of the room, but she stood behind the door out of his view. He leaned against the wall. "What, exactly have I done that you didn't ask me to? I didn't give the reporters those photos, if that's what you're thinking."

"Ben told me."

Helmut's heart froze in his chest. "Told you what?"

"About the bet," she continued, her voice growing quieter but firmer. "About how you were being groomed for CEO. You couldn't be the boss, so you screwed the boss instead."

"It wasn't like that—" Helmut hesitated. Wasn't it just like that? He'd pursued her in Chicago, and followed her to Paris. He'd drunk a toast to her seduction with Ben after he'd been fired.

"I hope you enjoyed your revenge. Now just go. Neither I, nor Sheffield & Fox, are your concern any longer."

Claire sat back against the cold metal door of the hotel room door, clasping knees to her chest as hot tears ran down her face.

Where did she get such wonderful taste in men? Claire swiped her cheeks with the sleeve of her designer jacket, not caring about the peach and black smears of makeup that trailed across the costly fabric.

He knew just when she checked out of the hotel. He heard the bellhop pushing a luggage cart down the hall, and caught a glimpse of bare calf as she stepped into the elevator. He had paced his room so long last night there was probably a groove in the carpet between the phone and the door.

He hoped she would call. Or knock. Or he should call. Or knock. Or call the concierge and have a dozen red roses delivered. Maybe a thousand roses. Did she even like roses?

Finally, sometime after three in the morning, he sat in an armchair and fell asleep. It was the sound of Cathedral bells from some nearby church that had awakened him. That, and the bustle of elevator buttons and shuffling feet in the hall as the other guests prepared to leave for the morning. Or to leave for good.

As the bellhop disappeared into the elevator behind Claire, Helmut closed his hotel room door softly.

What the hell did he do now? He had no job, had just insulted the daughter of the one man who'd offered business connections, and he had an expensive and empty suite in a posh Paris hotel for two more nights. Nights he had hoped to spend with Claire.

The growling of his stomach answered his dilemma for the short term. He quickly showered off the grime and sweat from yesterday's exertions and changed into a pair of jeans. He didn't bother to shave, but just grabbed his wallet and room key and made for the café across the street.

It was empty. Too early for tourists and too close to church time for the locals, he supposed. Helmut claimed a small table inside, away from the angry glare of the sun, ordered an espresso, and opened a two-day old Wall Street Journal he'd brought from the hotel. He flipped the pages absently, not paying much attention to the waiters bustling back and forth across the small room.

One stopped in front of his table. "Au lait, si vous plais," Helmut said, hoping that his high-school French was adequate for ordering cream.

"Sorry, fresh out," drawled the reply.

Helmut lowered the paper and looked up to find Ben looming over his table, not a waiter. Without asking, Ben pulled out a chair and sat down.

"You look like shit," Helmut said.

Ben had looked a bit messy on Friday, but today he looked like he'd been hit by a bus. One full of alcohol and wearing cherry-red lipstick.

"Same to you," said Ben, reaching into his pocket. He pulled out a roll of bills and tossed them on the table in front of Helmut. "There you are, all square."

Helmut shoved the money away. "Keep it."

Ben sneered. "Now don't get all high and mighty on me. I don't need a pair of wet panties to believe that you screwed Claire Sheffield. That little show you put on for the cameras was good enough for me."

"No thanks. Besides, you might want to watch your spending for a while," Helmut said evenly. "Until you get back on your feet."

The sneer turned into a grimace. "Don't fucking start with all your financial advice. I have a plan. I've been in talks for weeks with Arachnava. They don't give a rat's ass about the toy airplane problem."

Helmut set down his paper and frowned. "Arachnava? You're going to work for Frank Burwell?"

Ben grinned and picked up a sugar shaker. "You're looking at the new Chief Operating Officer, starting Wednesday. At about twice your, ahem, previous salary."

Helmut looked. And he saw his old friend, unshaven, unwashed, hair a mess and smelling like a cheap hooker. He shook his head sadly. "Do you have that in writing, Ben?"

"Can't you just be happy for me for once? Holy shit, what would it take for you to say 'Congratulations?' Or are you jealous of me this time?" Ben slammed the sugar dish down so hard the table rattled. Helmut cringed as the few other diners all stared their way.

"Ben, do you think Frank might have had ulterior motives in recruiting you?"

Ben shoved his chair back and stood up. He steadied himself briefly with one hand before glaring murderously down at Helmut. "Like trying to screw your girlfriend? What's the woman got in her pants anyway? A hoo-ha made of diamonds? Shit, I'm so wasted. See you around, loser."

Ben staggered out of the café, nearly tripping over a chair on the way. Helmut almost went after him. But in his present mood, there was nothing Helmut could say that wouldn't get flung back in his face. And he'd had more than enough of flying shit lately. Let Ben pick up the pieces of his own mistakes for once.

He contemplated the stack of bills. Even if he needed the money, he wouldn't keep it.

He heard church bells ringing as he drained the last few sips of harsh dense coffee from his cup. A thousand bucks was a hell of a lot more than twenty pieces of silver, but he knew where it might go to good use. And he left a generous tip behind him.

Chapter 19

Claire hesitated outside the door to her father's high-rise condo, fist raised at the knocker. Silly to hesitate, since the building doorman had to buzz her up.

She knocked. Firmly. And gulped. This would be one of the hardest conversations of her life, and she was not looking forward to it.

"CJ, come in," Father said with a smile as he swept the door open.

Claire set her purse down on the hall table and walked straight down the hall toward the living room. A wall of enormous windows gave a sweeping view of the Chicago skyline. Her father had selected this side of the building instead of a lake view on purpose. He always preferred the hustle of commerce to the serenity of the water.

"Can I get you a drink? A Tom Collins, or one of those fancy martinis that Diana's always drinking?" He walked over to the built-in mini bar and withdrew two glasses.

Father was dressed as casually as the man ever did, in creased khakis and a golf shirt. His salt and pepper hair was groomed, and a pair of supple suede moccasins served as his slippers.

Claire resisted the urge to smooth her own skirt, no doubt wrinkled from the cab ride over.

"No, Father, thank you. This is actually a business call."

"Business always goes better with a drink." He poured an amber liquid into a matching pair of cut-crystal double old-fashioned glasses and handed one to Claire.

She could smell the alcohol. Probably one of the whiskeys he preferred. She set it down carefully on the table.

"Father. James. I'm not here as your daughter. I'm here as the CEO of Sheffield & Fox."

He took a small sip of his own drink and raised one black eyebrow at her. "One and the same, my dear."

"No, they're not. And that's exactly the problem."

Her father sat down his own cup and motioned her toward the dove gray sofa. She sat, grateful that her knees wouldn't be able to knock. Unlike her nerves.

Her father sat opposite her and reclined back, hooking one ankle over the opposite knee. "I hope you're not still fretting over that mess in Paris last week. The press will die down soon enough. Now that the Air Force has declared the explosion an accident instead of terrorism, we can get back to solving the problems with the structure."

"Well, actually..."

"If you want my advice," her father continued. "Sack anyone still left from Lackey's team who knew about it. That engineer, Harriet, seems to have a level head on her shoulders. She could probably take over in the interim, if you pair her with a decent face-man."

Claire shook her head. "This isn't about Shadow Fly, Father. I signed Lackey's termination papers before I left Paris on Sunday. Along with one of his team leads. And the woman in accounting who signed a big check to one of the metal suppliers—without approval. I have an independent auditor already checking the rest of the books of the project. I have a feeling we'll be letting go of a few more people before we're through. But, it's covered."

James nodded his approval. "Good, good. Just what I would have done. Finally you're beginning to live up to your reputation."

Claire started. "My reputation?"

He smiled and swirled the amber liquid in his glass before taking another taste. "Did you know that I wasn't the one who threw your name into the ring for CEO? I wouldn't have even thought of it, if it weren't for a conversation I had with Chris Smythe—you know him, the director who flies in from Omaha for all our meetings."

Claire's mind was whirling. Her father hadn't handpicked her for the job? She didn't know whether to be relieved or ashamed.

"He apparently made a small fortune buying Arachnava stock at your IPO several years back, and holding it. Told me that every time he felt like selling, you'd change the company direction just slightly, and send the stock soaring again. He finally sold out after you resigned, and even with the drop in value right after you left, he set both daughters up with trust funds."

She shook her head in amazement. "I had no idea. He never said a word."

"No. Well. There are several of us who did pretty well during your run. And we all hoped you could breathe a little life into S&F, too. I thought I was making some headway with Shadow Fly, but my heart's just not in the business like it used to be. I used to lead the winds of change, not get blown around by them."

Claire bit her lower lip. "About Shadow Fly."

James drained the last of his cup. "If you need a few names for someone to help out Harriet, let me know."

"No, I don't think I will," Claire said softly.

"Hmm. Great. Who's the lucky guy? Or gal?"

Claire took a steadying breath. Here goes. "I canceled the project."

"You what?" James leapt to his feet.

"It is outside our realm of expertise. We had already sunk too many resources, and there was no possible way to expect that we'd make money off it. Ever. I think we need to refocus — "

"Of course we sank resources into the project. Do you know what it took to re-tool the site in St. Joseph? That was refocusing our business, expanding our markets." His face was turning a violent shade of red.

Claire stood up and laid a hand on her father's arm. "Please, calm down for a minute."

"Why hasn't the board heard of this?" he sputtered.

"I'm the CEO. I don't need board approval to curtail a program."

James stared at Claire, and she stared back, blue eyes to blue eyes. Finally he sat back down again. "You're right. But I still think you should have told me."

"I am telling you. And that's another thing I need to talk to you about."

He raised one eyebrow at her. Claire took her time, smoothing her skirts and arranging herself on the couch before meeting that challenge.

"If I weren't your daughter, would you think that I should be discussing the everyday operations of my company with you?"

"My company."

"No, the stockholders' company. And I know you're a majority shareholder. But my responsibility is to all the stockholders, not just the one I'm related to by blood."

James picked up his glass and stared at it, perhaps hoping it would yield more alcohol. He set it back down.

"I don't think it's a good idea for us to work this closely. As long as you sit on the board of directors, you will want a say in how the company is run."

"Naturally."

"And I won't be treated like a puppet. I am tired of the whispers and the snickers. In order to do my job, the employees have to feel that I can handle the responsibility to make the company work. Without asking my father for permission."

James opened his mouth and then shut it.

This was it. Claire's hands shook slightly as she folded them in her lap, and made a conscious effort not to squirm under her father's eyes. "One of us has to go, Father. One of us has to step down. You or me."

He was quiet for a long time, his face unreadable as always. The perfect poker face, an ideal businessman.

She had laid it out. She loved the challenges of Sheffield & Fox, but she could still walk away. Her heart wasn't in it, yet. Completely. Leaving Arachnava had been a thousand times harder. Leaving S&F would be almost a relief.

Almost, but not quite.

"I founded this company before you were born," James said at last. "We started out by buying and re-selling a single airplane. For the second one, your mother insisted that we reupholster the interior to make it look nicer, and we made twice the profit. By the time your brothers and you came along, we were custom-building them."

Claire knew the story by heart. Maybe not the bit about her mother, but about how her father had started with a small business loan and built an empire around the custom jet business.

"The last few years, the market's been tough. Business leveled off, then tanked. Diana's given up a lot of what I'd promised her. But we were scraping by. The Shadow Fly project was supposed to invigorate the company." He rubbed his hands over his eyes, smoothing his temples.

Claire stood up. It was time to go. "I'm sorry, Daddy," she whispered. She hadn't called him that since she was a girl.

Tears pooled behind her eyes and a sob choked her throat. This was harder. To fail, so publicly. To let her father down in front of everyone. His friends, his business associates, his trophy wife.

She got three steps before she felt his hand at her shoulder, keeping her from just leaving. "CJ, wait. Look at me."

Claire slowly raised her eyes to her father's, ashamed to let him see them red-rimmed and full of emotion.

"I am the one who should be sorry." His voice was low, raspy, and his dark blue eyes cloudy and gray. "I had no right to drop my problems on you."

She sniffed. "That's okay."

"No. It's not." He squeezed both of her shoulders in his hands and held her gaze with his own. "Claire, I screwed up. Shadow Fly was a disaster from the start. I appointed Lackey and he turned out to be barely competent. And I trusted Helmut Forrester—"

She started to open her mouth to protest, but Father cut her off.

"Don't be too hard on him. All that military and government stuff—it was a whole new arena. We didn't take the time to prepare, or even to read the rules. He made one mistake, that's all. It was my responsibility to catch it, and I let it slide. And brought you in to clean up my mess."

"We all make mistakes."

"And I know that you two have been involved. And I would be overjoyed to see that continue. Or not. I will stay out of it. I promise."

Claire tried to swallow, but there was a lump in her throat the size of a small helicopter. "I..."

"The biggest mistake I made was not stepping aside when we hired you. Claire, your leadership is already turning this company around. You made the calls that I couldn't. That I wouldn't."

Claire blinked. Did he say what she thought he just said? Her leadership? "No. It's your company..."

He shook his head with a sad smile. "No, CJ. It's not my company anymore. It's yours to run. I resign. Effective immediately."

"But what about the board? Your shares?"

"I didn't say I was selling out," he said with a roguish smile. "S&F is still my largest investment. And I'm trusting that you won't squander it all for me."

Claire's reply was smothered as he hugged her tightly to him. She struggled for a moment, and then relented and rested her head on his chest. He still smelled like she remembered, of Old Spice with that sweet-sour hint of whiskey.

"That's my girl," he whispered into her hair.

Chapter 20

"Mother, you are not fine," Helmut gritted out from clenched teeth.

Edna hobbled through the house, using one of his father's old canes to keep pressure off of her leg. She bent down and picked up Kelsie's dirty dinner plate from the kitchen table and balanced it in her free hand as she made her way to the kitchen.

"Give me that." Helmut snatched the plate out of her hands and swept past her into the kitchen, where his little sister was engrossed in a texting frenzy on her phone. "Kelsie," he warned.

"What did I do this time?" she said, not looking up.

"Take care of your own dishes. You know she can't resist chores."

With a quick thunk of the cane on the hardwood floors, Mother caught up to him. "I am perfectly capable of taking care of my own household and my children. I've been doing it for—how old are you?—forty years now. And I don't need another lecture."

Helmut rounded on her. Her head only reached his shoulders, but her stare gave her at least a foot high advantage. Or it would have, if she hadn't been wearing a bathrobe at three o'clock in the afternoon.

"I'm not buying it. You need rest. And a housekeeper."

She waved one hand dismissively. "It's only a sprained ankle this time. I'll be right as rain in a day. And I don't need some flighty young thing poking around in my garbage. I have one of those in my house already."

Kelsie clicked off her phone and stared, mouth agape. "Don't drag me into this. I just got here this morning."

Helmut crossed his arms over his chest. "My point exactly."

She slammed her phone down on the counter and poked a finger in Helmut's chest. "What crawled up your ass? You've been stalking around here all afternoon, slamming doors and complaining every time someone breathes the wrong way."

"I'm not the one leaving trails of shoes, purses, and dirty dishes in every room of the house. Someone has to take care of this family," Helmut thundered. Rage and frustration, hurt and sorrow boiled through him, threatening to explode.

"Mom was doing just fine before you swooped in to help."

"Just fine? She falls down a flight of stairs and is left all by herself for twenty-four hours before help arrives, and you think she's 'just fine?'"

Mother rolled her eyes. "You're overreacting, Helmut. I could have called for help at any point, but I didn't think it was a big deal. It's not like I was lying on the floor. And it's just a sprain."

"You didn't know that."

Helmut's mother drew back as his voice echoed off the hard cabinets and countertops of her kitchen. Even took a step back.

Helmut looked back and forth between his mother and sister, two sets of identical eyes staring at him with identically shocked expressions.

Edna recovered first, and her voice was calm and cold, ice and steel. The voice he had always half-feared, fully revered. "Helmut David Forrester. While you are in my house, you will speak to me and to your sister with respect. I might be old. I might be injured. I might not be as physically fit as I used to be, and I might forget where I leave my reading glasses. But I am your mother. And I raised you better than that."

The blackness that had wrapped Helmut's mood these past four days constricted around his heart and he saw himself for the tyrant he was becoming. With a guttural growl, he turned and slammed out of the French doors into the yard.

The sultry heat of the South Florida summer closed in on him, sun scorching the dark black T-shirt and jeans he'd donned that morning. The hot air was thick with the promise of a tropical storm, humid and heavy. It reminded him of a steam room. And of Claire.

With another growl, he took off at a run, toward the stand of trees at the back of his mom's property that led to the park. He slowed when he reached the untamed growth at the edge of the nature reserve. Branches slapped him in the face as he shoved his way through the green weeds and brush, and sweat dripped off his temples into his eyes.

He didn't think, just let his feet lead the way. The lush landscape had grown a lot over the past twenty-some years. But then he spotted it. A towering live oak, probably several centuries old, with sprawling branches dripping in Spanish moss. Helmut stopped and laid one hand on one of the trunk-like limbs, his heart pounding.

This had been his special hideout as a kid. He'd once woven a shade of branches and moss where he could stretch out with a comic book or a paperback or just a can of soda and his own thoughts. As a teenager, he'd brought a tent and sleeping bag out here more than once. And a girl or two.

Some of the upper branches looked broken, and one large limb was cracked and leaning on the ground, leaves withered and brown. As a kid, he'd thought the giant tree majestic. Now it looked old and battered from the barrage of hurricanes and tropical storms.

Helmut rested his head on one trunk. He knew how the tree felt.

When had he grown so old?

When he lost his fiancée. His father. When he married himself to his job. When he gave up on all but the most superficial friendships, the most casual flings.

Helmut slid down and rested his back against the trunk, fighting hot tears of self-loathing and self-pity. Had he really become so full of himself that he put his own needs before everyone else's? He didn't like facing the reality of that question.

Even his concern for his mother, and for Claire, was completely self-centered. He, Helmut Forrester, high-rolling daredevil, wanted to protect his loved ones for his own selfish needs. He was terrified of losing them.

At the sound of crackling leaves, he looked up and saw Kelsie, carefully picking her way through the brush. She stopped in front of him.

"Hey, big brother. Mind if I join you?" Without waiting for an answer, she found a wide exposed root and brushed it off before perching on the rough bark.

He raised one eyebrow. "You always go hiking in flip flops?"

She shrugged. "I didn't feel like checking the rest of the house for another pair of shoes. I'm going to need a pedicure after this, though."

"Heh." Helmut avoided her eyes, and stared at her feet instead. They were slender and groomed, and her toenails were polished with a very prim shade of pink. "What happened to purple and black?"

"I outgrew my Goth stage years ago."

"Doesn't seem that long to me."

She nudged his leg with one of those pink-tipped toes. "That's because you only see me a couple of times a year. A lot can happen between Christmas and the Fourth of July."

He studied her face for the first time in a really long time. Gone was the baby fat that once made her little cheeks so soft and round, and gone was her wide-eyed innocence. In their place were high, sculpted cheekbones and an intelligence that reminded him startlingly of Mother when she was younger. When he was younger.

"She didn't send me, you know," she said.

"Who?" he asked, already knowing the answer.

"Mom. I don't think she knows everything that's been going on."

Helmut sighed. "And what is it that you think is going on?"

She rolled her eyes, reminding him of her teenage self. "I read the news, Helmut. I saw those photos of you and Claire Sheffield in Paris.

And even Mom's heard about the explosion, and the investigation into Benjamin Lackey. He's one of your friends, isn't he?"

Helmut busied himself plucking a leaf off of a tall weed before he answered. Was Ben a friend? He didn't even know what that meant anymore.

"Claire's the one the flowers were for, isn't she?" Kelsie asked. "The date I interrupted in Chicago?"

Helmut felt his cheeks reddening. Good lord, he was actually blushing. He sat up and tore the leaf to shreds, and tried to cover his embarrassment with his deepest, most sincere-sounding big-brother voice. "Yes, Kelsie, Miss Sheffield and I were involved."

She kicked him in the shin again.

"Hey, little girl, it's a good thing those shoes are made of Styrofoam."

"Well, quit talking to me like I'm five. I'm not, you know. I've been in love before, too."

He raised an eyebrow at her. "You are too young to know what love is."

"How old were you when you met Olivia?"

"Twenty-one."

She crossed her arms across her chest. "I'm twenty-two, Helmut. I'm not too young. Maybe the problem is you're too old."

"What do you mean by that?"

"I saw the way Claire Sheffield looked at you at that baseball game. And at me. Until you introduced me, she thought I was your girlfriend. And let me tell you how glad I am not to have her as an enemy."

"Claire? She's harmless."

Kelsie snorted. "Do you even know anything about the woman? When she ran Arachnava, the woman was ruthless. She was smart, always positioning the company exactly where it needed to be for the next big trend about to hit. And she knew when to pull out and cut their losses. They didn't go from a garage to Fortune 500 by sheer dumb luck, you know."

"I didn't know you were such a fan."

"We studied her in a women-in-business course last semester." She gave a delicate shrug of her shoulders. Above the canopy of the tree, thunder rumbled.

Helmut contemplated Kelsie's words. In all of the time he'd spent trying to woo Claire over the past few weeks, he really hadn't bothered to look into her background. He knew she'd run the other business and done OK, and that she was James' daughter. He assumed that her parentage was what got her the job, not her experience. If Kelsie was right, he had underestimated her qualifications by a huge margin. And done not only Claire, but S&F, a huge disservice.

"Guess I deserve what I got then," he said.

"You mean getting fired, or having her dump you?" Kelsie rubbed her bare shoulders, and Helmut noticed a cool breeze blowing through.

"Both, I guess. I was a complete asshole." And then some.

This time, she just nudged his shin with her foot instead of kicking it. "What happened with that helicopter? Was it really terrorism like they said on the news?"

"Nah. Just poor management. Ben ran over budget then started cutting corners, thinking he could rake in the glory of the project. But it backfired on him. I told that to the investigators. That story will die out soon enough."

"Damn."

Helmut gave her shin a little nudge. "Hey, there, little girl. You watch your language."

She grinned at him, eyes gleaming. "Sorry. But you just cost me twenty bucks."

Helmut laughed as the first fat rain drops spattered into the high branches above them.

"We should get out of here before we get soaked," Kelsie said, glancing at the blackening sky.

"Yeah, we don't need Mom mopping the floors up after us." He hooked an arm around their shoulders as they started back to the house.

"Helmut, what are you going to do about it now?"

"I don't know. Hide the mop?"

She elbowed him hard in the ribs as they reached the edge of the lawn, then paused to pull off her flip flops. "Not about the floors. About Claire Sheffield? How are you going to get her back?"

The rain began to fall in earnest, sweet and cool on Helmut's face and arms. "I don't have a plan. Do you have any advice for me, little Miss 'Queen of Hearts'?"

Kelsie grinned. "Maybe. But you're going to have to catch me to find out what." She broke into a run across the green grass.

Helmut smiled as her long, slim legs tore up the space between where he stood and the glass of the patio door, remembering all of the races she'd challenged him to when she was still just a kid.

He continued slowly across the yard, remembering for a moment how life used to be, when he was in his twenties, with his first real-world job, dating a beautiful woman, and chasing his little terror of a sister around the park.

He would never get the years back, or the first love of his youth. But maybe he could find his way back to that happy feeling. One step at a time, he crossed the space back toward home.

Chapter 21

Claire set her glasses on the polished mahogany surface of her desk and rubbed her temples. Funny how the traditional style of her father's office furniture had grown on her over the past few months.

A message popped up on her flat-screen monitor, reminding her of her four o'clock appointment. Gracefully hiding all of the power and network cables had been one of her decorator's biggest challenges in updating the space for its new occupant. James Sheffield had preferred to keep his computing equipment tucked away out of site and to ask his assistant to print his emails, schedule, and reports. Claire had no intention of giving up that much control.

The intercom on her phone buzzed. "The rep from the U of Chicago is here."

"Thanks, Steph. Send her in."

"She's on her way. I'm headed out, Claire. I will see you in the morning."

"Have fun on your date tonight."

Claire slipped her glasses back on her face as she stood and smoothed the blouse she wore over her tailored slacks. She glanced around for the stylish pumps that complimented her outfit. She spotted them next to the reading chair on the far side of the seating area just as her door opened.

Too late. She'd have to conduct this appointment barefooted. It wouldn't be the first time.

Claire smiled as the woman crossed the fifteen feet from the door to her desk, glancing around the room in apparent appreciation. She looked around fifty-five, with graying brown hair and a plain, but pleasant, face.

"Miss Sheffield," she said, extending her hand. "I'm Maureen Glancy. It's a pleasure to meet you at last."

"And you. Please have a seat, Mrs. Glancy."

"Please call me Maureen." The woman smiled as she settled into one of the dove gray chairs opposite Claire. "I've never been in here before. Your office is lovely. All of that dark wood could look so imposing, but instead you have made it so very welcoming."

"Thanks." Claire glanced around. She had changed out the leather of the sofa and guest chairs for a crisp microfiber upholstery. Men could never appreciate how the bare backs of your legs stuck to chairs and sweated when wearing a skirt. And the fridge in the wet bar was now stocked with Diet Coke and bottled water instead of whiskey and imported vodka.

Maureen slipped a manila envelope onto the desk in front of Claire.

"You don't need to open it just yet. I want to start off by thanking you, on behalf of the University of Chicago, for your company's generous support. As the director of development, I like to meet with our donors in person, if possible, about once a year. As you are aware, Sheffield & Fox has traditionally sponsored two students, one in the arts and one in engineering. I know I don't have to remind you how tough the economy is these days."

Claire nodded. Everyone in the company had felt the bite that their lower stock price had taken out of their paychecks. Of course, most of S&F's financial woes had more to do with losing their Shadow Fly contract than with the economy.

"Miss Sheffield, can I count on your company to continue its generous support of our scholarship program?"

"Yes. In fact, I would like to add a third scholarship."

Maureen sat back in her chair, surprised. "Why, that's wonderful news."

"I would like to add a scholarship for a business student. Ideally, for a woman entering the field."

Claire smiled as the other woman thanked her profusely, and warmed to the praise. She knew that Maureen's flattery and graciousness were well rehearsed, but she didn't care. This was her own idea, and she had diverted some of the CEO's own discretionary budget to fund it. In her father's regime, that money would have been used to woo customers with golf outings and sports tickets. That kind of marketing and goodwill were still important, but so was investing in the future. And she told Maureen exactly that.

"I could not agree more, Miss Sheffield. Now, inside that packet are the donor contracts for renewing your scholarships with the university this year. My office will draw up the papers for your new award right away so we can get it finalized and start putting your money to work."

"I am looking forward to it, Maureen."

Both women stood and they shook hands. Claire came around the desk and walked her toward the door.

"I have to say, this visit has been the highlight of my week. Most of my other appointments have gone the other way." Maureen stepped through the doorway and paused next to Steph's vacant chair. "Oh, Miss Sheffield, can I ask you a favor?"

"Sure, what do you need?"

"I always get so turned around in these big office buildings," Maureen said with a self-deprecating smile. "Could you point me toward Mr. Forrester's office?"

Claire's stomach did a flip flop at the name.

"Helmut Forrester?" She hadn't seen him in over two months now. Not since Paris.

"Yes, Helmut Forrester. I thought he was on the twelfth floor, or was it the thirteenth?" Maureen looked at her expectantly.

"May I ask why?"

"I have a packet of paperwork for him, too. Usually our office just mails it, but since I was going to be in the neighborhood, I thought I could save the postage. Every penny counts in my job." The woman smiled at her own joke.

Claire was dumfounded. After all of the bad press at the Air Show, she was sure that every citizen of Chicago knew all about the botched contract. And their affair. "Well, Mrs. Glancy, Helmut Forrester doesn't work here anymore. He left a couple of months back to pursue other opportunities."

Maureen's face fell. "Oh. I'm so sorry to hear that. I was hoping to say hello. His fiancée worked in our office in her undergrad years."

Claire's heart caught in her throat and she practically croaked her next words. "His fiancée?"

The woman nodded. "She was such a beautiful girl. And so talented musically, of course. Such a sad story." She paused, then visually collected herself. "Well, I guess I will be using that stamp after all. Thank you again, Miss Sheffield."

After the woman left, Claire quietly closed the door to her office and sank down in her desk chair. She contemplated her laptop. She had no claim on Helmut. Not an employee. Not a boyfriend, or even a lover. But whether he knew it or not, he still had a claim on her.

Over the past few weeks, no one at the office had mentioned Helmut. The man worked here for over fifteen years, and everyone acted as though there had never been another CFO before his replacement, a top-notch executive that they'd lured away from one of their much bigger commercial airline competitors.

Or maybe no one mentioned him in front of Claire.

It was normal for some conversations to halt when she walked in the door, but that was something every manager faced. No one wanted to get caught venting in front of their boss. But more than once in the past two months, Claire had suspected that she was interrupting gossip of a less professional nature.

She flipped open the screen. Human Resources records were kept online, and she had a password. But that data was confidential. Personal. When she was preparing to fire Helmut, she hadn't looked in his files. Then, she hadn't wanted to know if he had any blemishes on his record, any extenuating circumstances.

And now it was too late. He didn't work here. She had no right to dig into his life. But there was another option.

Fingers pounded furiously on the keys as Claire brought up a web browser and began searching.

Forrester was a fairly common name, but Helmut was not. And he hadn't been living like a hermit. He'd been written up in Aviation Week, in Business Week, in Forbes, in the Sun-Times. She found his name on a racquetball bracket at a club not far from the office, and even found him on the title to his condo in the city records. There were a few false hits, too, but it was easy to dismiss the logging safety equipment links.

Finally, she found a link to a campus newspaper article from the University of Chicago, dated more than a dozen years ago. Claire clicked on the link and read what appeared to be a tribute to a student who had passed away.

A sob caught in her throat as she read the words "...survived by her fiancé, Helmut Forrester, who was not injured in the accident." She highlighted the woman's name—Olivia Redbloom, how beautiful—and began searching again.

Olivia's life was not as well documented as Helmut's, and many of the links that Claire found were broken and out of date. But there was enough. Originally from a small town in Nebraska, Olivia had been a music student with a lot of talent. She had played and sung with a cover band who specialized in weddings, apparently worked as a waitress, and in the past year of her life been increasingly photographed on the arm of a young and serious-looking accountant. They had made a beautiful couple, with Olivia looking sweet but striking, and a young Helmut always gazing adoringly at her.

Claire found a short write-up in the newspaper's archives about the accident. Helmut had been at the wheel. She was thrown from the car. He sustained minor injuries. The police called him a distracted driver. No charges were filed.

Claire sat back and tried to reconcile the Helmut she knew with the staid-looking young man he had been. She checked the date of Olivia's obituary. Helmut would have been about twenty-six or twenty-seven.

At that age, Claire and Frank were still deeply in lust for each other and their startup company. They were busy and focused, and dreaming huge dreams of the future. Marriage was a far-off concept, at the bottom of the ever-growing to-do list. It never made it very high on the list.

What had Helmut been dreaming at twenty-seven? Of his future with the musician? Of marriage and a family? Would he have been a hands-on kind of father or the kind who was married to his work, as Claire's father always had been. Would his youthful love for Olivia have survived a corporate career, or would they have been another divorce statistic, trading kids every other weekend the way Claire and her brothers were traded?

He'd never had the chance to find out. Instead, his thirties had been full of press releases, golf outings and benefit dinners, with a different woman on his arm at every photo op. The life he lived sounded a lot more glamorous and carefree on paper. And in the company gossip.

But the man she knew held a lot more emotion in reserve. She remembered the way he had made love to her after their own small car accident in Paris. The haunted look in his eyes, the desperation in his kisses, in his touch. There was nothing carefree about the way he had held her that afternoon. Claire shivered.

Maureen Glancy said that Helmut donated a scholarship to the school. Claire searched the website one more time and found a link to the Redbloom Memorial Scholarship. Founded eleven years ago in memory of one Olivia Redbloom.

Helmut hadn't attended that concert last spring on behalf of Sheffield & Fox.

Claire leaned in and studied the face of this year's recipient. He looked vaguely familiar. She searched for his name and found him right away on MySpace.

"Heh," she said out loud as she read his latest update. "So long, Mr. Hon. Thanks for all the egg drop soup." Stevie was the Chinese food delivery boy from her favorite restaurant. And he'd apparently been offered a plum job composing for Disney.

"We ordered from the same place," Helmut had told her that first night in her office. She closed her eyes and remembered how she'd spilled sauce on her blouse, and been mortified — and turned on — when he'd helped her clean it up.

Claire spun around in her chair, surprised to see orange rays of sunset sneaking around the buildings of the Chicago skyline. She hadn't meant to stay so late.

On impulse, she picked up her phone and dialed Helmut's home number. She regretted it the moment she hit the last number. What would she say to him when answered? *Hi, I was googling you and found out all about your past.*

The phone rang on the other end.

She could tell him about Maureen Glancy's visit. It was a weak excuse, but it was the best she had. Maybe he would want to get together for a drink and talk?

The phone rang again. Maybe he wouldn't answer.

But someone did.

"Hello?"

Claire's heart seized. The voice was female, and youngish. Would he have a housekeeper? At eight at night? But it was too late. Her number was on the caller ID, now. He'd know it was her.

"Is Helmut there?" *Please tell me it's the wrong number.*

"Um, no. Can I take a message?"

Claire exhaled. "No, thanks."

"You're calling from Sheffield and Fox, right?" the woman asked. "Is it about the paperwork he's waiting for? Helmut said that if HR called to tell you to forward it to his Florida address."

Claire almost smiled. Of course she'd called from her desk phone, not her personal cell, and the caller ID always showed up as something generic. But it gave her the opportunity to pry a little further. "Um, great. Can I get your name? I have to, um, record who I talked to. For the record." Geeze that sounded lame.

"Sure. This is his sister, Kelsie Forrester."

Claire felt like kicking herself. His sister. That was the second time she'd let her jealousy take over about Helmut's *baby sister.*

"Thanks, Miss Forrester. Let him know that we'll be in touch."

She hung up the phone and popped open another web browser. Kelsie had mentioned an address in Florida. With a few clicks she had it. Big Pine Key, Florida. Helmut owned a beach house.

Chapter 22

Helmut bent to brush off the sand clinging to his bare calves from this morning's stroll along the beach before entering Java Joint. Sam, the owner, always made a fuss of sweeping the entry way behind the tourists who wandered in from sunbathing for their caffeine fix. To call the crusty old man a barista was still a stretch, but over the past year, he'd at least learned how to brew a decent latte, and he had recently added Wi-Fi, in the fashion of all those "Yankee" coffee shops.

"You want the usual?" Sam asked, looking up from the spot of stainless steel countertop he'd been polishing.

Helmut nodded and shoved his sunglasses up onto his head, his eyes still adjusting to the shift from the blinding sunlight outside. He walked automatically to the table closest to the counter, and therefore farthest from the windows that lined both the beach and the highway sides of the small café. The glare of sunlight made his laptop screen nearly unreadable.

Sam began turning levers and pushing buttons on the espresso equipment behind the bar with a flourish and a mutter that sounded suspiciously like, "Come on, baby."

Helmut's lips quirked in a grin. Whether the shop owner would admit it or not, Helmut thought he liked the trappings of a "Yankee" coffee shop. Helmut pulled his laptop out of the canvas messenger bag he wore over one shoulder and booted it up.

"She yours?" Sam asked, sliding Helmut's cup to the edge of the serving counter where Helmut could reach it.

"The coffee?"

"No, the girl." Sam jerked a thumb over his shoulder toward the street-side windows. "I don't think she's taken her eyes off you since you walked in the door."

Claire.

The morning light pouring in from the east highlighted the edges of her golden hair, glowing like a halo that framed her face and rested on deliciously bare, toned shoulders. She wore a long white washed-linen sundress that fell to just above her knees. Dangling from one bare toe was a hot pink flip flop.

The shoe dropped softly from her foot, falling to the floor soundlessly. Heat flowed to Helmut's groin as he remembered picking up that same shoe from the steam room floor. Carefully he cleared his throat and raised her gaze to Claire's eyes.

Slowly she stood and walked toward him, hypnotizing him with the way her dress flowed around her legs, clinging to her hips and her breasts. As she got closer, he saw the ties of a string bikini at the neckline to her dress instead of a bra. His lips went dry.

She stopped inches from the edge of his table, her blue eyes wide and unsure. "I asked at the hotel where I could get a decent cup of coffee. I had a feeling I might find you here."

Helmut smiled and found his voice. "You got lucky. I'm having a satellite dish installed later this week. Then I'll be able to work without walking over here every morning."

"Hey, you didn't tell me that," Sam said from behind Helmut.

"Sorry, Sam. I'll be back for the coffee, though. Sam, this is Claire. She's a, er, friend of mine from Chicago."

Sam gave a wave from behind the counter and set to work washing a blender. One that Helmut was sure had been clean just sixty seconds ago.

Claire's eyes darted to the café owner and back to Helmut questioningly. "Can we talk for a minute?"

"It's such a beautiful morning. Why don't we take a walk on the beach." Helmut jumped to his feet and hurriedly packed his laptop back away. He motioned for the door and stopped a few feet away, then rushed back and tossed a five dollar bill on the counter next to his still-steaming coffee.

He almost grabbed it, but outside, the temperature was already pushing ninety. Too hot for coffee. And Claire's unexpected arrival made him feel jittery enough.

She stopped at the edge of the sand and kicked off her sandals, then slipped them in a tote bag she had on her shoulder. Wordlessly, she followed him as he took off across the beach, past sunbathers already slathered with oil.

She broke the silence. "So, you have a vacation house down here?"

"Yeah. I rent it out most of the year." In the sunlight, that white dress was nearly transparent. He gulped.

"Mmmm," she said. "It's beautiful here. Are you're thinking of staying?"

"How did you know I might be staying? Oh yeah. The satellite. When did you arrive?" The sand was getting hot, and he walked closer to the edge of the tide where the cool gulf water could cool his feet.

"I flew in last night."

"You drove down from Miami this morning?" he asked.

Claire giggled. The sound bubbled over Helmut, and his gut ached. God how he'd missed her smile.

"It turns out," she said teasingly. "That I happen to work for a company that manufacturers small private jets. And the company even owns one or two that employees can use. With executive permission, of course."

Helmut raised one eyebrow. "Figured that out, did you?"

"Of course I'll have to pay all costs. This isn't exactly a business trip."

He stopped and dug his toes into the sand, allowing the cool water to wash over them. She stood so close now that her long hair tickled his face as it blew in the breeze. He lifted a small lock to his nose and inhaled the sweet scent of coconuts before tucking it behind her ear. "Why are you here?" he asked softly.

Claire's eyes were wide pools of Caribbean blue, her pupils dilated, her lips parted just slightly. Helmut's body was all too aware of her nipples, peaked and visible beneath her dress and swimsuit, and the soft rise and fall of her breasts as she breathed. Just a touch too fast.

"Come on." He took her by the hand up beach toward his house. Despite the hot morning, her fingers were cold in his, and he felt her tremble lightly as he guided her to the stairs leading to his front door, high off the ground.

He pulled her inside the house into the cool air conditioning. He put one hand on the inside of the door, above her shoulder, positioning her between his body and the steel of the door. He closed it gently, and touched her hair again, then stroked her cheek, and she closed her eyes at the caress.

After two months of hell, she had arrived, looking like an angel in white. A temptingly sexy angel. Slowly, he leaned in toward her, letting the body heat from her breasts warm first his T-shirt, then scorch his chest. He slid one knee between hers, and lowered his lips until they almost brushed hers, then stopped there. "Why are you here?" he asked again, dreading the answer, but needing to hear it anyway.

She looked up at him through her lashes, her temples pink with heat. Her fingers found his chest and traveled upwards, leaving trails behind like footsteps in the sand, until they found his shoulders.

Blood pulsed through Helmut's cock, straining at his khaki shorts, but still he waited. The move was hers to make.

And move she did.

She snaked her fingers through his hair and drew his lips to hers with a sudden fierceness. Helmut's hands left the door to wrap around her and cup her butt, pressing her against his erection. Their lips clashed and tangled, both greedy for the taste of each other, both impatient.

He pulled on her skirts, bunching them up around her waist so that he could feel the bare skin of her hips and thighs with his fingers. He found the strings that held the sides of her bikini closed and tugged one bow free.

Claire groaned as he lifted her knee upward and wrapped it around his waist so that he could explore her with his hands. She was wet. Slippery. Hot.

Helmut trailed kisses across her face to her ear as he teased her clit and he felt her shiver and nearly lose her balance. He had to adjust their stance so that he held her firmly against the door, and his body complained as it put space between the two of them.

But then he slid two fingers into her, and she moaned and writhed, and he could set aside his own need to watch the emotions and pleasure play across her beautiful face as he stroked her. Deep and swirling. Lightly brushing her clit with his thumb, and then harder.

She moved against his hand, urging him higher, harder, more. Until he felt her contract around his fingers and still briefly.

"Helmut," she whispered, her eyes stormy. He slowly removed his hand and swallowed her protest with his kiss. He then lifted her other leg up and around his waist and carried her.

The heat of her sex rubbing against his cock, still trapped inside his pants, was tortuous as he walked across the living room to the bedroom and his bed. He lowered her bottom to the edge of the bed and with a quick jerk of his arm swept the covers onto a pile on the floor.

He sucked in his breath as she worked the button on his shorts. Then her fingers — no longer cold — hit the bare flesh of his abdomen. She yanked his shirt upwards, and he swept it up and over his head while she unzipped his pants. He gritted his teeth as she pulled his cock free and rubbed its hard length with her hands, then her tongue.

Helmut pulled back and kicked off the rest of his clothes. "Now yours," he said.

She pulled her dress off over her head, and the bikini bottom was already gone, lost somewhere between here and the front door. That left her sprawled on his bed, wearing only two tiny triangles of fabric and some string.

Helmut knelt and kissed her bare belly button, flicking his tongue around her navel and grasping her hips in his hands. She sucked in her breath in anticipation, but he moved his mouth and hands higher, not lower. He kissed her sternum and slid up her ribcage and around to her back.

He sucked first one nipple, then the other, through the fabric. She arched her back pressing more of her beautiful breasts to his mouth, and allowing him to untie her top. With his thumbs he brushed the scraps upwards, exposing her nipples. And then rubbing them. Up, down, his thumbs worked the sensitive flesh until she was panting and rubbing her pelvis against his thigh.

He slipped the top up and over her head and then kissed her again, and pressed his full weight down on her. His cock rubbed against her wet opening, and she pressed her breasts against his chest.

With a groan, he found a condom in the nightstand and then he was inside her. She wrapped her legs around his waist and lifted her butt, allowing him full access. Helmut thrust deeper, harder. She kissed him hard on the mouth, thrusting her own tongue into his, echoing his thrusts into her hot center.

She wanted more. He got up on his knees, pulling her hips up off the bed so that he could penetrate as deeply as possible. She looked exquisite, with her hair arrayed around her head as she thrashed with pleasure. Her entire torso was bare to his view, and to his touch. He cupped her breasts with his free hand, and then reached between their bodies to rub the pad of his thumb over the nub of her clit.

Claire cried out, and he repeated it, rubbing in time as he stroked his cock in and out. In and out. She arched, and he changed the motion of his thumb, swirling it faster as he controlled the strokes until she was begging, her legs locked tight around her back.

"Please," she begged and their gazes locked. Her eyes were glazed with passion and pleasure.

Helmut closed his eyes as he brought them both to their climax. As her contractions rippled over him, his own poured forth. The power of it scared him.

Chapter 23

Claire yawned and stretched as she looked around Helmut's bedroom. The furniture was simple: a bed with no headboard, a whitewashed dresser, a chair with a pair of jeans draped across it. But the water view was spectacular. One entire wall was made of windows with French doors leading out to the same deck she had crossed on her way in the front door.

He was there, leaning on the railing, staring out at the sea. How long had she slept? After making love, they had lain together quietly, limbs entangled, both lost in their own thoughts. Both afraid to speak for fear of shattering the perfect silence.

She was still reeling from the surge of *something* that had washed over her when she saw him this morning in the coffee shop. That something was so hard to name. Happiness. Desire. Excitement. Peace. *Rightness*. That was the word. It felt so right to walk next to him, to be in his arms, in his bed.

She had no idea what kind of welcome she would get when she found him. Anger. Scorn. Or worse, indifference. Instead, it was that unreadable glint in his eyes. Passion underscored by something else. She gave herself a mental shake. It was probably just lust. She wanted the something else, looked for it.

Because, God help her, she was in love with Helmut Forrester. Friend of her father's. Jaded playboy. A man of questionable ethics, living life in the fast lane. That's what everyone told her, what she was warned about from day one.

But that nifty little portrait didn't quite fit the man standing in front of her at the railing. The one who donated anonymous scholarships and nursed an ailing mother. The one who stood up a date with a sure thing to help out his kid sister. The kind who cradled her body with his to protect her from an explosion.

Claire sighed and swung her legs over the edge of the bed, scanning the floor for her discarded dress. She had thrown away almost a decade on Frank, deluding herself that the man loved her when really he was living off of her. Like a tick, he had sucked her confidence and energy and grown fat. And insanely hard to get rid of.

And Helmut? He had stood behind her, supported her, helped her, protected her. He didn't try to claim her success for himself.

She didn't bother with her bathing suit, and slipped the gown over her head.

Then there was the childish bet with Lackey. Once her temper had cooled, and she had a few thousand miles between herself and Paris, she'd turned Lackeys' words over and over. Helmut had not collected on that bet before leaving Chicago for Paris. Despite the steam room. And making love in her apartment. And being fired.

Claire opened the door a crack and stepped out into the afternoon sunshine. The house faced west, and the sun hadn't yet rounded the corner from the south, so the pale wood under her feet was hot but not scorching, and the sun was bright but not blinding.

"Hi." She took a spot at the railing next to him.

"Hey."

They stood there for a long moment, each staring off over the ocean as the soft lapping of water washed over them. Claire struggled for how to begin. How do you go about telling a man you're in love with him? She couldn't even remember how she'd broached the topic with Frank. First things first.

"I made a statement to the board of directors," she said.

He turned toward her then, and leaned one elbow on the railing. "About what?"

"About our relationship. I gave them the truth about when it started. The real truth—that we were personally involved before you were asked to leave." As the words tumbled out of her mouth, she felt a weight lift.

"Huh. What did your father say about that?"

She shrugged. "I don't think he minded. It doesn't matter, anyway. He retired. But not because of us."

His look penetrated her thoughts, and she blushed. "Well, he did go because of me. I told him that I couldn't work with him and keep the respect of the employees. I offered to leave."

He smiled, his eyes crinkling at the corners of his tanned face. "But he left instead. That sounds like him."

"I wouldn't have thought so," she muttered.

"Really, why?" He looked genuinely surprised.

Claire shrugged again. "The James Sheffield I grew up with was ruthless and selfish. If he wanted something, he went after it. No holds barred. He didn't care whose feelings he stomped on to get it."

Helmut put one hand over hers. "It must have been rough being his daughter. I remember some of the ruthless, as you put it, days, too. But I think he mellowed the past few years."

"Apparently." She looked down at their hands, hers paler and pinker against his, strong and tanned from a few weeks in the sun.

"And I made a hugely public scene about Frank. Had him escorted out of Sheffield and Fox's lobby one day. I threatened him with a police order of protection if he kept harassing me. I think that finally woke him up."

Helmut gave her hand a little squeeze. "He always struck me as a bit spineless. Has he been back?"

She shook her head. "He never has liked confrontation. And after my father stepped down and he realized that I wasn't going anywhere, I think he gave up. I hope he did."

"He and Lackey deserve each other."

She nodded. "We're still investigating all of the Shadow Fly finances. But so far it just looks like a case of gross mismanagement."

"Ben always did take the easy road. I should have paid more attention to the signs early on. You were right to fire me, you know. I wasn't fit for that job."

"Oh, I don't know. Half the company still sings your praises."

He raised one eyebrow. "Only half?"

She grinned. "The male half. The female half are either too pissed at me or too heartbroken over you to sing anything."

Helmut winced and stepped back, letting Claire's hand drop. "I never set out to break anyone's heart. I just—"

"You don't have to explain yourself to me. I knew who you were from the beginning," she said quietly.

His gray-green eyes turned stony again. "Claire, I'm glad you're here. But I don't think it's a good idea for us to keep seeing each other."

Claire's heart constricted. This was what she was afraid of. "I told you once that I don't need anything complicated."

His eyes flicked over her face, searching her features for something. She smiled bravely. Coolly. But in her heart, she knew this was a losing battle. This was his MO. When a woman declared herself in love with him, he ran. Not that she blamed him.

"That's the problem, Claire. With you, things are already complicated."

She shook her head, denying his words. Grasping at anything. "It doesn't have to be. I know it's been a mess. And I know you don't want a woman to get too close. But I can—"

He closed the distance between them in one step and cut off her words with a searing kiss. When he finally relented, she was breathless.

"I'm sorry," he said, pressing a kiss to her forehead.

A sob formed in Claire's throat, and she squeezed her eyes shut, focusing every nerve on his body still so close to hers. She wanted to memorize his scent, his warmth. "I am, too. God,

Helmut, I know it's the last thing you want to hear. But if we're over, what can it hurt?"

"What's that?" His voice sounded strangled.

"I lied to you just now." The words were almost a relief. She didn't know if the twisting pain in her chest would ever heal, but at least she could walk away and not regret that she held back. She pressed her hands to his chest, willing her fingers not to curl themselves into the soft fabric of his shirt. Willing them not to cling. "I...I'm glad you refused my offer. Because I don't think I can be here, with you, without complicating things. I love you. And I'm not sorry that I came. Only sorry that I have to go."

She tried to step back, tried to turn around, but he refused to let her go.

"What did you say?"

She gave another shove, and he wouldn't budge. She fought back the tears that clogged her throat. *Don't back down.* She forced herself to meet his eyes. His look was hard and intent. His breath was uneven, and there was a hint of a flush beneath the scruff of his chin. She wanted to run away, but that would not resolve anything. She knew that now.

"Never."

"I love you, Helmut Forrester. I love the way you make me laugh. I love the way you take care of your family. I love that you donate that scholarship to the university in memory of your fiancée. I love that so much that it hurts. I wish that you could love me that deeply, that long. And most of all I wish..."

He didn't really flinch, not physically. But she saw in his eyes how he shut down. It was like a door slamming, with her on the wrong side. Just like she'd done to him in Paris.

She drew in a ragged breath and licked her parched lips. "But I am not her. I should leave."

His grip on her arms softened, but if anything he drew her closer. "No, you are not her."

"I am nothing but a complication."

He closed his eyes for a moment and when they opened again, they were brimming with an intensity that made Claire's knees weak. "Olivia is gone. She has been gone for a long time. She will always be in my heart, but time moves on. Things change. I changed. I don't want another Olivia in my life."

Claire nodded sadly.

He smiled, slow and seductive. "I said that, with you, things were already complicated. I'm in love with you, Claire Sheffield. I have been since Paris. Not because you are just like Olivia. Not because you are completely different than Olivia. I love you for who you are."

"But I thought you didn't want complications." She opened her mouth to speak, but words refused to form.

"You took the job that I thought I was ready for and showed me that I could never have handled it. You fired me and kicked me out of the hole where I had buried my all my feelings for years. You seduced me with your intelligence. And with your honesty. And with those incredibly long, sexy legs.

"I want you. All of you. Complications and all, and I won't accept any less."

Clare stared, open mouthed, until Helmut leaned down and kissed her. Kissed away her doubts. Kissed away her breath. Kissed away her self-control. Kissed away all thoughts of goodbye.

The End

About the Author

A voracious reader since before she can remember, Kristi has always been drawn to romance, science fiction, and fantasy, or, preferably all three at once. Now, when she isn't reading her favorite books to herself or to her kids, she is writing her own stories. Kristi, her husband, and their two children live with a pair of cats rescued from the streets of suburban St. Louis.

Visit her online at www.KristiLea.com

Also by Kristi Lea

Affairs of the Heart
      The Christmas Affair, Volume 1.5
      The Vegas Affair, Volume 2 *Coming 2016*

Accomplice

Call the Rain

www.ingramcontent.com/pod-product-compliance
Lightning Source LLC
Chambersburg PA
CBHW020633260626

47157CB00008B/2714